"No! I've never slept with him!"

Nickie realized she was almost shouting and struggled to contain her anger.

A murmur passed through the courtroom. "Never?" Marieli's attorney demanded. "Remember, Ms. Brinton, you are under oath."

Nickie took a deep breath. "As God is my witness, I've never slept with Miguel Aldabe." *But not because I didn't want to....*

"Ms. Brinton, isn't it true that you both used your research as an excuse to be alone with each other, away from everyone—his fiancée, his—"

"Objection!" Nickie's lawyer said fiercely. "The witness has already stated emphatically that she and Miguel Aldabe did not sleep together!"

"Sustained."

"Your Honor," Marieli's lawyer said smoothly, "I submit that adultery is first entertained in the mind."

"Objection!"

"Overruled." The judge leaned toward Nickie. "Ms. Brinton, explain your relationship with Miguel Aldabe...."

Dear Reader,

Bride of My Heart is my third book about Nevada men and the women who love them (after *The Rancher and the Redhead* and *The Mermaid Wife*).

Miguel Aldabe, the hero of this story, is of Basque descent. *Basque* is a French word, also used in English, describing a group of people who live in both Spain and France in areas bordering the Bay of Biscay and the western foothills of the Pyrenees. The Spanish term for Basques is *Vascos*. But native Basques refer to themselves as *Euskaldunak* and their language as *Euskara*. It's unrelated to any other spoken language in the world.

My interest in the Basque people began years ago with an incident my husband and I experienced when we were driving in the Uinta Mountains of Utah. Our truck stalled. We were miles from help so we started walking out and ran into a Basque tending sheep. He was very kind and fed us a delicious meal, then drove us to a ranger station. To this day, I can still picture him in that isolated mountain setting: handsome, friendly, self-reliant and completely comfortable with nature.

Since then, I've learned about the great contribution Basques have made to the settling of the American West, particularly in the states of Utah, Idaho, California and Nevada.

I wish to thank Ms. Linda White, assistant coordinator of the Basque Studies program at the University of Nevada, Reno, for all her time and invaluable assistance. And many thanks go to Mr. Marcelino Ugalde, library assistant, and Ms. Joan Brick for answering my thousand and one questions. I also wish to thank Mr. John Bodger for his assistance with information pertaining to Nevada Law.

I hope you'll enjoy this final romance about Nevada heroes!

Sincerely,

Rebecca Winters

BRIDE OF MY HEART
Rebecca Winters

Harlequin Books

TORONTO • NEW YORK • LONDON
AMSTERDAM • PARIS • SYDNEY • HAMBURG
STOCKHOLM • ATHENS • TOKYO • MILAN
MADRID • WARSAW • BUDAPEST • AUCKLAND

ISBN 0-373-03325-7

BRIDE OF MY HEART

Copyright © 1994 by Rebecca Winters.

CHAPTER ONE

"NICKIE? I'M GLAD *you* answered the phone. Are you alone?"

Something in her mother's question filled Nickie with alarm. "Aunt Charlotte and Uncle Richard are still out to dinner, but they'll be home soon. Mom? What's wrong? Does this have anything to do with Dad or the kids?"

"No, honey. Everyone's fine."

"Irene then?"

Nickie heard the slight hesitation in her mother's voice and she started to panic. "I-is this about Miguel? He's not..."

"He's asked Marieli for a divorce," her mother said.

Nickie was so relieved to know Miguel was all right it took a few seconds for the words to register. When they did, she thought her mother must be joking. "That's impossible," she murmured in a daze. "Divorce? On what grounds?"

"Incompatibility."

Incompatibility? Nickie had grown up around the Aldabe family and knew Miguel's marriage to Marieli had been arranged by their grandparents back in the Basque country years earlier. Miguel would never break up their home, would never bring that kind of dishonor to the family. "You must be mistaken, Mom."

"I wish I were, honey. Unfortunately, Marieli is countersuing and there's going to be a trial next week."

"*What?*" Nickie's hand tightened around the receiver. "There's never been a divorce in either family. I don't believe it!" Basque couples stayed together. That was their strength. Husband and wife held their marriage sacred. If Miguel divorced Marieli, it meant he had turned his back on his entire heritage, everything he stood for.

"Nickie. Please listen for a minute. There's more, and it has to do with *you*."

At those words a cold, clammy sensation crept over Nickie's skin. She thought she was going to be sick to her stomach, and she sank into the nearest chair.

"Nickie? Honey?"

"I'm here, Mom."

"As part of the grounds for the countersuit, Marieli has brought a charge of adultery against Miguel, and her attorney has called you as a key witness."

"*Adultery?*" A fresh surge of adrenaline drew Nickie to her feet. "*Miguel?*" She let out an angry laugh. "Marieli actually thinks Miguel is capable of committing adultery? Mom, he's the most honorable man I've ever known." Her voice throbbed as she struggled to repress certain memories that would always haunt her. "She must be insane to believe such a thing, or to expect me to testify against him!"

"Honey. You've misunderstood me. Oh, I wish there was an easy way to say this. Marieli has named *you* as the other woman."

"Dear God!"

"Before you say anything, you need to know that your father and I have been to Carson City, and we've retained a reputable attorney to handle your case. His name is Jason Helm. As soon as Irene found out about the charges, she came to see us and told us to call him. He's the lawyer who helped Governor Cordell's son when he was in serious legal trouble with that drug problem a few years back. He'll be able to handle whatever Marieli's attorney tr—"

"I can't do it!" Nickie broke in. "I came to Colorado to get away from Miguel and his family. I couldn't face him or Marieli again, not after what happened."

"I'm afraid you don't have a choice. That's why I'm calling now. Tomorrow morning, a constable will be serving you a subpoena, and I want you to be prepared."

Nickie felt as if she'd just been flung into a dark void. "You don't understand. I don't think I could live through a trial, Mom. Did you tell Mr. Helm that? Does he know what happened last January?"

"Yes. Your father and I gave him as much information as we could. He has real empathy for you. He said he could set up a hearing with the judge before the trial to try to get you excused. But he also said that because of the nature of the complaint filed, the judge will order you to testify, anyway, and we'll have gone through a hearing for nothing. He feels it would be best if you just complied and got it over with."

Nickie hid her face in her hands, the receiver dropped awkwardly against her hunched shoulder.

"Your father and I want you to fly home as soon as you've received the summons. There's a prepaid ticket waiting for you at the Continental counter at the Denver airport. Your flight for Reno leaves at 6:28 tomorrow evening. We'll pick you up."

She could hear her mother discussing the travel arrangements, but Nickie was too shattered by the unexpected news to really listen. "What am I going to do?" Her voice was a strangled whisper.

"You're going to face this knowing your mom and dad are one hundred percent behind you. When you get home, you'll meet with Mr. Helm and work out a strategy. You're to keep a low profile until the trial. He told us to refrain from discussing the case with anyone. He's very relieved to hear that you've been out of state."

"How could she do this, Mom? *Why* would she do it?"

"Certainly money is a motivating factor. She's asking for ten million dollars in punitive damages, plus the house and the lakefront property."

Aghast, Nickie cried, "But she came to the marriage a wealthy woman! She doesn't need more. Why would she drag all our families through a hideous trial? That kind of publicity will rock the Basque community—and the whole town—for years to come."

Besides the pain this trial would cause her own family, Nickie didn't even want to think about the impact it would have on Miguel, who was an intensely private person. The notoriety could damage his career and everything he'd been working for.

Nickie's mother answered briskly, "The fact that Marieli is countersuing in such an ugly, vindictive way, with total disregard for you and your reputation, reveals a very sick, insecure, grasping woman. If this is the real Marieli poor Miguel's been married to all this time, it's no wonder Miguel has broken with tradition to divorce her."

"I knew she hated me, but to go this far, to hurt Miguel needlessly... What kind of proof does she think she has?"

"Mr. Helm gave us a copy of the complaint. I have it right here. Do you want me to read it?"

"No—" Nickie gasped. "Yes."

"It's long and full of legal jargon, but I'll read the counts that pertain to you. It says, 'Marieli Echevarria Aldabe and plaintiff were never able to settle into a happily married life because of Nickie Brinton's relentless, willful and intentional actions to destroy their relationship, not only throughout their troubled marriage, but long before the marriage ever took place.'"

Nickie had known the charges would sound horrible, but to hear the fallacious words, to realize they were actually put to paper for everyone connected with the case to read, was pure agony.

"Honey, there are thirty documented pages of evidence pertaining to times and dates when you and

Miguel were together. Too many for me to read over the phone. Let me just finish these other two counts.

"'Ms. Brinton's adulterous relationship with the plaintiff has caused the defendant to suffer severe emotional distress, loss of intimacy, companionship, support and affection within the marriage relationship.

"'Because of Ms. Brinton's actions up to and including the night of January third, the plaintiff Miguel Aldabe filed for divorce, thereby breaking the prenuptial agreement entered into by both plaintiff and defendant, an agreement to bond both parties forever and to protect their futures. Because of the adulterous relationship, which brought about an end to the marriage of less than two years' duration, in the which time said defendant did not work outside the home in order to have a baby, defendant is therefore entitled relief and prays judgment as—'"

"Don't read any more, Mom," Nickie begged. "I wish I were dead."

"You're not to talk this way, Nickie. We know it's all lies. And nothing in life is so hopeless that you should ever feel that desperate."

"You weren't there that night, Mom. You didn't hear the venom that came out of Marieli. You didn't see the way Miguel looked at me," she said as the scalding tears that had been dammed for so long rushed down her pale cheeks. "The anger—" *The anger and the pain....*

"Nickie? That's all over. And soon the trial will be over, too, and you'll be free to get on with your life."

"I've made a life here."

"Selling sporting goods in your uncle's store is hardly the life you were meant to live. The trial could turn out to be a blessing if it helps you face your fears."

"I'm not strong like you, Mom. A-as soon as the trial is over, I'm coming right back here. Now that it's September, Uncle Richard's business is picking up and he needs me."

"Don't make any rash decisions. As for Richard, he can always hire someone else. You're much stronger than you know, and one day you'll come to believe it. *If* you'll give yourself a chance."

"I wish I had your faith," Nickie half sobbed. "I'm sorry my problems have hurt you. This attorney must be costing you a fortune. I'll repay you somehow."

"Honey, right now the important thing is to get you through this."

Nickie broke down completely and it took a minute before she got herself under control. "I don't know what I'd do without you and Dad."

"We feel the same way about you. Give our love to Richard and Charlotte. Tell them we'll call as events unfold. And we'll see *you* tomorrow night. Hurry home, honey. Eight months is far too long to wait for a hug from my daughter."

"ALL RISE. The Second District Court of Wahoe County, Reno, Nevada, is now in session, Judge Wilford R. Memmott presiding. You may be seated."

From where she sat outside in the hall, Nickie caught that much of the bailiff's pronouncement before the doors of the courtroom closed and she couldn't hear anything else. Jason Helm sat down next to her on the bench. The sixtyish, gray-haired attorney reminded her of a seasoned United States senator—sophisticated, immaculately groomed and exuding confidence.

"Let me explain what's going to happen," he said. "Miguel Aldabe will be put on the stand first to state his case. After cross-examination, Marieli Aldabe will go on the stand. When she has put forth her case and been cross-examined, Mr. Aranburu will call you as his first witness. I want you to stay out here until it's time to testify.

"Remember what we talked about earlier. He's going to paint you as a predatory female out to ensnare Miguel Aldabe any way you could. He'll make it nasty and he'll be cruel. But you're going to show the court what a calm, intelligent, high-class woman you are. You'll answer his questions as briefly and as honestly as possible. Remember, shorter is better, and no emotion."

"I'll try," she whispered.

"Good. And keep in mind that Mr. Aranburu won't be able to prove adultery. Even if the claim were true and you confessed to it, it wouldn't matter to the court. This is a community-property state and the assets will be divided equally. The adultery charge is a vicious, vindictive tactic to sensationalize the trial and inflict as much pain as possible on Miguel and on you, but it won't rally sympathy with the judge."

No. It will only make lifetime enemies of all the Basque friends I've come to know and enjoy over the years, Nickie lamented silently.

He reached into his briefcase and pulled out some papers. "While you're waiting, look these over. If there's any ground we haven't covered or some information you forgot to tell me, write it down. I'm going inside now and I'll call you when it's your turn." He patted her hand. "You're going to be fine."

Nickie nodded, and once he'd left, she spent the next hour reading over the evidence meant to prove that she and Miguel had carried on a love affair both before and during his marriage to Marieli. The thirty pages of documented times and places took her back though the years and looked so damning she broke out in another cold sweat. No one reading or hearing these charges would believe she was innocent, that Miguel had never touched her except in a brotherly way. *Not once...*

"Nickie? Marieli and Miguel have finished stating their cases. You're next."

At the sound of her attorney's voice she lifted her head in shock. She'd been so immersed in bittersweet memories, she hadn't realized how much time had already passed. As she got to her feet, that familiar knot of dread tightened in her stomach. "I—I'm afraid nothing of importance came to mind." She handed him the papers.

"That's all right. Let's go."

Nickie nodded and kept her eyes straight ahead as she followed him into the courtroom. If she looked anywhere else she would see the hostile, accusing stares of Basque friends and acquaintances—the relatives of both parties—who filled every available seat.

She purposely avoided glancing to her left where she knew Marieli was seated at a table with her wiry dark-haired Basque attorney. To her right, Miguel conferred with his lawyer, a trim dark blond woman in her midforties, smartly dressed in a business suit. Again he'd surprised Nickie by choosing a non-Basque to represent him.

Nickie refrained from looking at Miguel. Never again would she allow the angry blaze of those black-brown eyes to scorch and wither her.

When she took her seat in the front row next to her parents, her father squeezed her hand and murmured, "I know you're scared, but just tell the truth. And remember that you're an innocent bystander who became a victim in someone else's tragic marriage."

Nickie kissed her father's cheek, drawing strength from his encouraging words.

"Counsel for the defense calls its first witness, Nickie Brinton, to the stand."

"Good luck," her mother whispered. The love and trust in her parents' faces brought a measure of calm to Nickie's soul. Squaring her shoulders, she moved toward the witness stand, determined not to break under any circumstance.

After she was sworn in and seated, she glanced for the first time at her inquisitor. Mr. Aranburu's small dark eyes, set in a gaunt narrow face, studied her openly. He stared at her face and honey blond hair shaped in a blunt cut. Then, with a cold look that was obviously meant to intimidate, Marieli's attorney deliberately scrutinized Nickie's well-proportioned figure which she played down with a tailored three-piece ivory suit.

Here it comes. Clasping her hands so tightly together they actually hurt, Nickie fought to keep her composure.

"State your name."

"Nickie Marr Brinton."

"How old are you?"

"Twenty-five."

"Where do you live?"

"In Colorado Springs, Colorado. But before that, I lived with my parents at Incline Village, Lake Tahoe, Nevada."

"Are you employed?"

"Yes."

"Where do you work and what do you do?"

"I work at the Timberhaus in Colorado Springs and I sell sporting goods."

"How long have you been employed at the Timberhaus?"

"Eight months."

"And before you left the state, how did you occupy your time?"

Nickie took a shuddering breath. "Before I left, I was a full-time graduate student at Reno City College, studying the Basque language and culture. And during the summers, I worked at the Biscay Inn in Carson City as a waitress."

"Doesn't the Aldabe family own that restaurant?"

"Yes."

"Isn't it true you've worked there every summer for the past nine years?"

"Yes."

"Except for the summer before last, Ms. Brinton. You couldn't have forgotten you were on a study-abroad program at the University of San Sebastian in the Pyrenees—with Miguel Aldabe."

"I went with Miguel's sister, Irene. We stayed with relatives of the Aldabe family."

"You mean you went an entire summer without seeing him?"

"Objection!"

"Sustained. The court will not tolerate sarcasm, Mr. Aranburu."

"I apologize and will rephrase my question. At any point that summer, did Miguel Aldabe join you?"

"He came for three weeks in July."

"To teach?"

"No. To do research."

"Isn't it true that he stayed at the same home where you and his sister were residing?"

Nickie's eyes closed tightly. "Yes."

"Isn't it also true that you and Miguel Aldabe left his relative's home for ten days to travel—alone—in the Pyrenees?"

Was there anything he didn't know? "Yes."

"Did Irene Aldabe go with you?"

"No."

"Why not?"

"Because she wanted to stay in town and visit with old friends."

"Were you aware that Marieli Echevarria lived in Irun with her parents and brothers?"

"Yes."

"Were you aware that she and Miguel Aldabe were engaged?"

"I knew there was an understanding, but the subject never came up. I was there on a working vacation. My professor in San Sebastian is a close friend of Miguel's. They wanted me to accompany Miguel while he did some research in several mountainous regions. The Basque language can differ from valley to valley, and they wanted me to take full advantage of a unique opportunity to learn as much as I could while I was there. In fact, my professor joined us for four of those days."

"Isn't it true that you and Miguel Aldabe started sleeping together from that period on?"

Nickie's cheeks blazed like a hot furnace. "No!"

"How many times have you traveled to the Basque country with Irene Aldabe?"

A haze of unreality surrounded Nickie. The attorney's voice sounded as if it were coming through a tunnel. "Three times."

"Tell us about the first time. How old were you?"

"Seventeen."

"What were the circumstances?"

"It was the first of June, right after high school let out. Irene and I flew to Paris with Miguel. We rented a car and toured France and Spain, then drove into the Pyrenees where we stayed with their relatives in Irun."

"They're a generous and very wealthy family aren't they? They're one of the wealthiest families in the state of Nevada."

Adrenaline surged through her body. "My family and I paid for every—"

"Objection! This line of questioning is ludicrous."

"Sustained. Confine your remarks to the pertinent issues, Mr. Aranburu, or I'll find you in contempt."

"Yes, Your Honor. Ms. Brinton, Miguel Aldabe was present on all of those trips, wasn't he?"

"Yes."

Nickie bowed her head and closed her eyes, wishing the vivid memories of that incredible time—those years when hero worship slowly changed to something else—didn't still bring her pain.

"Speak up, please."

"Yes," she said a little more loudly.

"That's better. Isn't it true that on your third trip to the Pyrenees, Irene Aldabe became ill and was confined to a relative's home?"

"Yes."

"When did your third trip take place?"

"During winter break at the college here."

"And isn't it also true that you and Miguel Aldabe left the Pyrenees and spent a week together in the Republic of Georgia in the Caucasus?"

"Yes."

"How old were you?"

"Twenty-three."

At the outburst of noise, the judge pounded his gavel. "Order in the courtroom or I'll ask the bailiff to clear it."

The attorney waited a moment, letting the murmurs subside into silence. He glanced once at his client, then turned toward Nickie and began again.

"At that time, Ms. Brinton, were you aware that Miguel Aldabe had an understanding with Marieli

Echevarria? That, in fact, he was there in Irun ostensibly to finalize the arrangements for their wedding, which occurred two months later?''

"I didn't know he was there for that particular purpose, but ever since I met the Aldabe family, I've known that one day Miguel and Marieli would be married. It was decided by the families years ago. Arrangements were made for Irene's marriage, as well.''

"Are you telling the court that Miguel Aldabe purposely kept information about his imminent wedding plans from you?''

Jason Helm leapt to his feet.

"Objection! He's leading the witness.''

"Denied. Answer the question, Ms. Brinton.''

"Miguel never had any reason to discuss his personal life with me. We're eight years apart in age, and I'm Irene's friend. It just so happened that he had important business in Tbilisi and he'd made arrangements ahead of time for me and Irene to accompany him. He'd planned to visit a colleague, another professor, who had a married daughter. She intended to show Irene around while Miguel, the other professor and I worked together. Unfortunately Irene came down with the flu and was too sick to travel.''

"So the two of you flew to the Caucasus, leaving his sister and fiancée behind. Did the two of you spend all your time in the company of Dr. Aldabe's colleague?''

Nickie's throat felt constricted. "We would have, but just before our arrival, his family was involved in a serious car accident, which prevented him from accompanying us.''

"Under the circumstances, did you and Miguel Aldabe return immediately to the Pyrenees so he could be with his fiancée?"

Nickie's heart fluttered so fast it felt as if a thousand butterflies were trapped inside her. "No."

"Tell the court what you did do."

"We did research at the university there and traveled to some areas Miguel wanted to visit, not only as part of his project, but to help me find material for my thesis. At the end of each day, I'd type up our notes to prepare for the next day's work."

"How did you travel?"

"By rental car."

"Where did you stay at night?"

"At various hotels."

"Just the two of you?"

"Yes."

"Did you sleep in the same hotel room each night?"

"No. We had separate rooms."

"Your Honor, may I introduce in evidence Exhibit C, which is a copy of the receipts for six nights spent at various hotels in Georgia, as well as northern Turkey. All of them show that only one room was paid for each night."

How did Marieli's attorney manage to know every little facet of their private lives?

The judge pounded his gavel to quiet the immediate surge of noise in the courtroom.

"Ms. Brinton, I'll ask you again. Did you sleep in the same room with Mr. Aldabe?"

"No. In all cases, there was a connecting door between our two rooms. They were so small I assume at one time they were one room, and were at some point converted into two."

"Were there two entrances to the rooms?"

"No."

"So you had to go through one to reach the other."

"Objection."

Mr. Helm spoke in a weary-sounding voice. "This line of questioning is irrelevant. One room or two—it doesn't matter. Sharing the same room doesn't necessarily mean sharing the same bed."

"Sustained."

"Ms. Brinton. Did you sleep in the same bed with Miguel Aldabe during any portion of that trip?"

CHAPTER TWO

NICKIE STRUGGLED to contain her anger. "No! I've never slept with Miguel."

A murmur passed through the courtroom. "Never?" Aranburu demanded. "Remember, you are under oath."

Nickie took a deep breath. "As God is my witness, I've never slept with him."

But not because I didn't want to. . . .

Visibly angry, the attorney said, "Are you aware that when Marieli Echevarria learned Miguel Aldabe intended to take you to Georgia with him, even though Irene Aldabe couldn't accompany you, there was a bitter argument between them?"

Nickie hadn't known that. She averted her eyes. Had Marieli wanted to go on the trip, anyway? And if so, why hadn't Miguel allowed her to?

"Ms. Brinton? Answer the question."

"No. I didn't know." The only reason she could think of for their argument was that Marieli had no interest in academic subjects and probably didn't like Miguel's preoccupation with his career. He'd probably realized she'd be at a loss in a strange country where she couldn't speak the language. To Nickie's certain knowledge, Marieli had few interests outside the home and would have been lonely in a miserable hotel room while she and Miguel were doing their research.

But if Nickie had had any idea of Marieli's growing jealousy back then, she never would have gone on that trip with Miguel.

"Ms. Brinton, you've said that he took you along to do his typing, but surely he could have brought back notes for you to type up later on. Isn't it true that you both used that trip as an excuse to be alone with each other, away from everyone—his fiancée, his sister, his—"

"Objection!" Mr. Helm said fiercely. "The witness has already stated that she and Miguel Aldabe did not sleep together! Furthermore, she has also testified that she was planning to use this research in the future, for her own thesis. At the same time, she was assisting Dr. Aldabe with his project."

"Sustained."

"Your Honor," Aranburu said, "I submit that adultery is first entertained in the mind."

"Objection!"

"Overruled." The judge leaned toward Nickie. "Ms. Brinton, explain your working relationship with Dr. Aldabe, and tell us what was in your mind when neither of you returned to the Pyrenees after learning of the car accident."

Heat enveloped Nickie and she bowed her head. Only God knew the indescribable joy she had felt when she'd learned that she and Miguel were going to be alone together for ten whole days.

Clearing her throat, she said, "When I first became friends with Irene years ago, I also became interested in her Basque heritage. They're marvelous people, hardworking sheep ranchers and restaurateurs, and they've contributed so much to the growth of Nevada.

"Working at the Aldabe family restaurant was like being in a foreign country, and I loved it. All day long I heard patrons speaking Euskara, their native tongue, plus smatterings of French and Spanish, and I envied them their linguistic abilities. Miguel—Dr. Aldabe— was already a professor of Basque at Reno City College, and his enthusiasm was so contagious that my fascination with the Basque culture grew and flourished.

"When I started college and spoke with the incoming freshman counselor about my interest in the Basque language, he advised me to get as broad a base in foreign languages as I could. He suggested I go for a double major in Spanish and French, with a minor in Euskara. That way, I'd be prepared for several graduate programs in case I changed my mind at some stage.

"He didn't want me to rule out the possibility of pursuing Arabic and the Coptic languages, either, because of increasing research opportunities in those areas.

"Miguel concurred with the counselor's advice and helped me map out my course work. He said he'd do everything possible to expose me to Euskara, so I'd know if it was the career choice I really wanted. We had long talks about it, and he explained that there were infinite research possibilities concerning its origins.

"Contrary to what the general public believes, Euskara is not a derivative of French or Spanish, though the Basque country is nestled between France and Spain. He told me about a theory advanced by a world-renowned linguist at the University of Bordeaux, René Lafon, who believes there's a connection between Euskara and the language spoken in Georgia.

"That theory captured my imagination, and Miguel said that one day I could write a thesis on the subject and he'd help direct it."

She inclined her head toward the judge. "If you're looking for an underlying motive for my wanting to spend time in Georgia's libraries learning how to do research under Miguel's guidance, then that's it, I guess. It was an unparalleled opportunity for me.

"You have to understand that those familiar with Euskara and Basque culture recognize Miguel Aldabe as one of the world's foremost authorities in this field. These past few years, he's been in the process of putting together a definitive text on the Basque people—their origins, their culture, their language.

"Writing a textbook is a huge effort, especially for someone like Miguel, who has so many other responsibilities and demands on his time. He heads the College's Basque department, which means he's in charge of curriculum. He's constantly adding acquisitions to the library, plus he advises foreign students, speaks at seminars around the world *and* teaches his classes.

"When I began at the college, Miguel asked me if I would organize and type the notes he'd started on his book. I agreed because I wanted as much exposure to Basque as possible and I needed the money. Then I served as a liaison with hundreds of people of Basque origin whom he'd interviewed for firsthand information. As time went on, he trusted me enough to start looking up specific material for him."

"Give the court an example of the work you did," the judge ordered.

She took a deep breath. "All right. When we were in Tbilisi, in Georgia, I would find books on a local dialect and look up columns of suffixes and prefixes, so I could study the syntax and compare it to modern and ancient Euskara. Miguel would use my notes, and it left him free to do the more difficult research. Each step exposed me more and more to the language. By the time I entered graduate school, I had enough background to start my thesis, and I subsequently received a research fellowship.

"I've been very fortunate to work with Miguel. He's a tremendously busy and important man, Your Honor. He's sought after by other institutions to chair their language departments. But he's chosen to stay in Reno. To work for such a scholar has been enlightening, and a privilege." Nickie finally ended her little speech, surprised and embarrassed that she would have defended him so energetically when he'd hurt her more than any other person alive.

An odd smile broke out on the judge's face. "Thank you for your articulate insight, Ms. Brinton." Then he turned to Mr. Aranburu. "Counsel may proceed."

Marieli's attorney was staring daggers at Nickie. "Ms. Brinton, let me take you back to your third visit to the Pyrenees. Are you aware that when Marieli Echevarria learned of the car accident, she offered to join her fiancé in Georgia immediately but was told by him unequivocally that she was not to come?"

Nickie shivered. "No. Since he didn't discuss his personal life with me, I wouldn't have known what went on between the two of them."

"Like an ostrich who puts its head in the sand, you display an astonishing facility for ignoring what you don't want to see and pursuing your own agenda whether it brings pain or not."

"That's not true—" Nickie cried as Mr. Helm got to his feet.

"Objection. Mr. Aranburu's opinions are irrelevant."

"Sustained."

"You were a third-year graduate student at Reno City College. Did you hold a job during your school years?"

"Yes."

"Where?"

"At the college."

"What was your job?"

"I worked in the library and helped with the cataloging of new books and periodicals."

"Which library would that be?"

"The Basque Institute's."

"Who got you that job?"

"I applied for it."

"I believe you've already indicated that Miguel Aldabe is the head of the Basque Institute?"

Nickie moistened her dry lips. "He's the director, yes."

"When did you start that job?"

"When I entered as a freshman."

"Do you still have that job?"

"No," she murmured, remembering how she'd felt the day Miguel came to her without any warning and said another person had been hired to work in the library. "In November I was replaced by someone with more experience and transferred to the Romance-languages department where I did secretarial work."

"What degrees do you hold?"

"A B.A. and an M.A."

"And you are pursuing a Ph.D. in the Basque language?"

"I was working toward one, yes."

"*Was* working?"

"I'm no longer enrolled at the college. I—I've changed my plans," she stated quietly.

"You mean to tell the court that after a long-term investment in studying the Basque language you're no longer pursuing a career in it? You stretch the court's imagination beyond its limits, Ms. Brinton. Who was your instructor?"

"I've had several."

"I have your transcript in front of me, Ms. Brinton. It shows that Miguel Aldabe has been your teacher for most of the graduate credit hours you've received so far."

Nothing in her life was sacred. Nickie gripped the side arms of the chair as a wave of dizziness passed through her. "I also had classes from Ana Guevera and John Forrester."

Marieli's attorney pivoted to face the judge.

"Your Honor, Reno City College is one of the only institutions that offers a Ph.D. program for Basque studies in the Western world. Thus the court must conclude that if Nickie Brinton chooses to continue her career—the career she's worked toward for years—she will have to remain in close association with Miguel Aldabe. There's no other way to complete her doctorate."

He took a drink of water, gazing at Nickie from hooded eyes that reminded her of a reptile's. "You mentioned John Forrester. Is he married?"

"When I last saw him, no."

"How well do you know him?"

"Not well."

"Would you say he and Miguel Aldabe are close?"

"No."

"Does Miguel Aldabe have any close friends besides you?"

Nickie didn't know if she could control her anger. "Of course. Mr. Zackery Quinn, for one. Governor Andrew Cordell—"

"Objection. Calling for a conclusion," her attorney broke in.

"Sustained."

"Has Mr. Forrester ever asked you out on a date?"

"Yes."

"Did you go?"

"No."

"Why not?"

"Because I wasn't interested in Mr. Forrester that way." *Besides, no one compared to Miguel. No one....*

"Isn't it true that Miguel Aldabe *told* you not to go out with him?"

"No. Not specifically."

"I have a notarized affidavit from the assistant director of Basque studies, Mrs. Guevera, that says Miguel Aldabe did have such a conversation with you."

Nickie's nails bit into her palms. "When Mr. Forrester first asked me out, I felt uncomfortable because, though I had no desire to date him socially, I had a job in the Basque library. I wanted to keep up a good working relationship with him, as well as the other faculty members and graduate students.

"I mentioned my concerns to Irene, and I assume she told Miguel. At one point he took me aside and warned me in his capacity as head of the department that it wouldn't be wise to get romantically involved with any member of the faculty while I was still a matriculated student. That must have been the conversation Mrs. Guevera overheard."

"Mrs. Guevera states that you and Miguel Aldabe argued over it. Why did you argue?"

Nickie remembered that painful moment as if it were yesterday. After telling her she had been replaced, Miguel had warned her about dating other men in the department, as if she'd done something wrong. "B-because I never had any intention of dating Mr. Forrester or anyone else in the department and didn't want or need anyone's unsolicited advice on the subject. I was sorry word had ever reached his ears about it."

"What is obvious to the court is that Miguel Aldabe considered you his private possession, expected your exclusive adoration and couldn't countenance your having a relationship with any other man."

Nickie let out a shuddering breath. *If only that had been the truth.*

"Objection!" Jason Helm bellowed.

"Sustained. You're close to being in contempt, Mr. Aranburu."

"I apologize, Your Honor. Ms. Brinton, do you have a boyfriend?"

Nickie wanted to crawl into a hole. "Not at the moment."

"Have you ever had a boyfriend?"

"I've dated, if that's what you're asking."

"I'm asking if you have ever had a steady relationship with a man over a period of weeks or months or years."

"No." *Not when Miguel filled my mind and heart to the exclusion of any other man.*

"Except for Miguel Aldabe, of course."

"Objection."

"Sustained."

"Tell the court about your relationship with Irene Aldabe. How would you describe it?"

"We're very close."

"And how would you describe your relationship with Miguel Aldabe?" he asked with heavy innuendo.

Nickie tried to swallow, but couldn't. "I've known him for a long time." He'd been her whole world for years. She couldn't even remember a time when he hadn't been.

"How long?"

"Irene and I have been best friends since third grade."

"Since you are now twenty-five years old, the court can assume you've known him eighteen years."

"I've known the Aldabe family that long. Yes."

"Where did you live when you attended the college?"

"In a house near the campus."

"Who owns the house?"

"It's one of the rental houses owned by the Aldabes."

"Did you live there alone?"

"No. I shared it with two other girls."

"Please give the court their names."

"Irene Aldabe and Amaia Echevarria."

"Amaia Echevarria? Please tell the court who she is."

"She's a cousin of Marieli's. The Echevarria family has members both in Irun and in Nevada. They're very close-knit."

"How long did you live at that residence while you attended college?"

"Except for summers, I suppose we lived there seven years or so."

"I have the figures on the home, which is located in one of the high-rent districts. Houses of that square footage are normally rented at anywhere from $1000 to $1400 a month. Split three ways, the least amount you'd be required to pay would be $333 a month. How much rent *did* you pay a month?"

"We didn't work it out that way."

"Who is we?"

"Miguel."

"Then how did you work it out?"

"Neither Amaia nor Irene paid rent. My portion was taken out of my college paycheck every month."

"How much was that?"

Nickie felt her heart stop for a moment. "A hundred dollars."

There was a swell of murmuring, then it quieted.

"What you are saying is that you were supplied virtually free accommodation over a seven-year period?"

"No. I'm not saying that. He refused to take any more money from me because he said I more than made up for the rest by helping him with his book when I wasn't working at my job or on my own studies."

He pounced like a cat. "What you're really saying is that you slept with Miguel Aldabe at every opportunity, thereby ensuring that you would be kept in a style to which you'd become accustomed."

"No!"

"Objection! The witness has already testified under oath that she has never slept with the plaintiff."

"Sustained."

"Ms. Brinton, did Miguel Aldabe ever come by the house in that seven-year period?"

"Yes."

"How often?"

"I don't recall."

"I have an affidavit signed by Amaia Echevarria that says he was a frequent visitor, often dropping by six, seven times a week, generally in the evenings—even after his marriage to Marieli Echevarria."

"I wouldn't know the exact number of visits because I spent so much time on campus. But it's certainly possible, since he and Irene are very close and he has always watched out for her and protected her."

"Has he ever asked you to tend his baby?"

"No."

"Yet in the same affidavit I just mentioned, Ms. Echevarria states that you tended the baby on several occasions at the rental house."

"That's because once in a while, when Miguel dropped by with the baby to see Irene, I happened to be home and volunteered to baby-sit if they wanted to go out somewhere together."

"Did he make a habit of bringing the baby with him?"

A sea of faces stared at her with icy contempt. But it was Miguel's penetrating gaze she refused to acknowledge.

"I don't remember. He might have brought the baby over four or five times in total."

"It's obvious to the court that along with an eighteen-year personal family association, Miguel Aldabe has been your friend, teacher, mentor, landlord, employer, adviser and lover."

"Objection."

"Sustained. Strike the word 'lover' from the record."

"Were you present at the wedding of Marieli Echevarria and Miguel Aldabe?"

"No."

"Why not?"

"It was for family only. I wouldn't have been invited."

"Was there a party held for the couple a week before the wedding?"

"There were many parties going on all month."

"How many did you attend?"

"Very few."

"Why?"

"Because most of them were private family parties given by relatives of the bride."

"What about the party given by Zackery Quinn, a friend of Miguel Aldabe's? Did you attend that party?"

"Yes." Nickie fought to keep the tremor out of her voice but it betrayed her.

"Where was the party held?"

"On the Circle Q ranch."

"Did John Forrester attend that party?"

"Yes," Nickie answered in a dull voice. She couldn't stand John Forrester and wished she'd never heard of him.

"Objection, Your Honor. My client has already testified that she did not want and did not have a romantic relationship with Mr. Forrester. Counsel's reference to him and this line of questioning are redundant and pointless."

"Your Honor," Aranburu responded, "my client has accused her husband and this witness of adultery. I'm attempting to show the court how the constant and relentless presence of Ms. Brinton in Miguel Aldabe's life has resulted in this case being brought to trial. Mr. Forrester plays a pivotal role in this denouement, as I will prove if the court will allow me to proceed. With regard to Dr. Aldabe and Ms. Brinton, we're not talking a few months, but years and years of intimate contact and association that caused untold mental anguish to my client."

"Objection! The word 'intimate' implies a sexual connotation that has not been established."

"Sustained. Strike it from the record. Get to the point, Mr. Aranburu."

"Ms. Brinton, did you dance with Mr. Forrester at the party?"

"Yes. One dance."

"Did the two of you have an argument?"

"Yes."

"Would you summarize for the court what it was about?"

"He told me he'd been patient long enough and hoped I'd relent and go out with him. When I told him I considered him a friend, nothing more, he accused me of being infatuated with Miguel."

"What did you say to that?"

"I told him Miguel was like a brother to me, and that in any event, it was none of his business. Then I walked away from him."

"Did you see or talk to him again that night?"

"No."

"Did you see or talk to Miguel Aldabe that night?"

"Yes."

"At any point during that party, were you alone with him?"

With her heart pounding in her ears she said, "Yes."

"Tell the court the circumstances."

"Toward the end of the party I went for a swim in the pool with friends. Later, Zack—Mr. Quinn—and Miguel joined us. It happened that Miguel and I were the last ones out of the pool. We talked for a few minutes, then I went to my room. *Alone,*" she emphasized to save him the trouble of asking.

"Did the two of you kiss while you were in the pool?" A strange light glittered in his eyes.

"No," she whispered, suffocating from haunting memories she'd tried to suppress since that night but couldn't.

"Remember you're under oath."

"I could hardly forget, Mr. Aranburu."

"Let's move forward to the night of January third of this year, approximately eight months ago. While you were at the Aldabe residence tending the Aldabe baby, you entertained John Forrester in that home. While the two of you were otherwise occupied, the baby became ill and—"

"Objection!" Jason Helm stormed to his feet. "Counsel's statement is libelous and slanderous. No charge of negligence was ever brought against the witness. And in any case, it's not the issue of this trial!"

"Sustained. Mr. Aranburu, must I remind you these theatrics do not belong in a court of law?"

"I'll start again. Please tell the court in your own words how you came to be at the Aldabe house. Did Marieli Aldabe ask you to baby-sit their daughter on that night?"

"No."

"Did Miguel Aldabe?"

"No."

"Then how did it happen that you ended up tending their baby without their permission?"

Nickie cringed inside, not daring to look at Irene who sat in the front row of the overflowing courtroom between her mother and father, surrounded by all their Basque relatives.

"Miguel asked Irene to baby-sit for the entire night. She agreed, but at the last moment something came up—she had to go out for a few hours. So I offered to watch the baby until she could get back."

"Unbeknownst to the baby's parents, isn't that correct?"

"Yes. When I arrived at the house, they'd already gone out for the evening."

"Has Marieli Aldabe ever asked you to baby-sit for her?"

"No."

"Wouldn't it be true to say that you would be the last woman on earth she'd ask to watch her baby?"

Nickie wondered how much more she could take before she collapsed in pain.

"Objection! Counsel is calling for an assumption on the part of the witness."

"Sustained."

"Tell the court what happened when John Forrester appeared at the Aldabe residence. Had you invited him?"

Memories swamped her and sickness welled up in her throat. "No."

"What was his reason for being there?"

"I thought he'd come to see Miguel on business. When I told him Miguel and Marieli were out, he said that didn't matter because he'd actually come to see me."

"How did you react to that?"

"I was surprised and annoyed. In the first place, I had no idea how he'd found out I was there." Nickie paused to take a steadying breath. "I told him I wasn't interested and I started to shut the front door. That's when he said something that disturbed me a great deal.

"Against my better judgment I let him into the house, because I was afraid that if we stood at the door, I wouldn't be able to hear Katalin. Just before the bell rang, I'd checked on her and discovered she was asleep and that her temperature was down. You see, earlier in the evening she'd been fussy and feverish from a slight cold. I realized she could wake up any time and start crying."

"What did Mr. Forrester say that was so upsetting to you?"

"He said he knew the real reason Miguel had fired me from my job in the library. When I asked him how he could know anything that confidential, he said he was close friends with the Echevarria family and had learned they'd put pressure on Miguel to let me go because they felt I was trying to break up the marriage."

"Did you believe him?"

"No."

"Why not?"

"First of all, I happen to know Miguel wasn't happy with my work. Th-that's why he let me go." She fought to keep her voice steady. "Secondly, John lost his credibility with me when he suggested we start dating to show her family and everyone in the department that the gossip was unfounded."

"So, in other words, you refused to believe there might be some truth to what he said, and you decided this was a ploy on John Forrester's part to get you to go out with him."

"Yes. I told him he was wasting his time and to please leave me alone. I was so disgusted I warned him that if he ever approached me again outside of a professional setting I'd write a formal complaint against him and submit it to Miguel."

"Did he leave after that?"

"No. He started apologizing. He said he was sorry for upsetting me and that he'd hoped for a different outcome. He said . . . he said a lot of things that really aren't important now."

"What things?"

"They're personal. I'd rather not say."

"Answer the question, Ms. Brinton," the judge prompted.

Nickie squirmed in her seat, embarrassed to have to relate the details, especially when John was in the courtroom, listening.

"He told me he'd fallen in love with me and that he couldn't get me out of his mind. He'd hoped that with Miguel married and unavailable, I would see him in a new light. His confession embarrassed me and I told him he'd have to go because I needed to look in on Katalin."

"Did he leave?"

"He started to, but Marieli and Miguel returned unexpectedly and walked in on us."

"What happened then?"

This was the part she dreaded telling. The part that had changed her life forever. "While Miguel showed John out, Marieli turned on me and demanded to know Irene's whereabouts.

"When I told her Irene had to leave for something important and I'd offered to look after Katalin until she could get back, Marieli asked me how I dared enter her home when I was Miguel's mistress, how I dared entertain another man when I was supposed to be watching her baby. It was then I realized that John had been telling me the truth. Marieli actually believed I was involved with Miguel.

"I tried to explain about John being there, but she ignored me and went upstairs to check on the baby. That's when I heard her scream. Katalin's temperature had soared. She was burning up and—" Nickie broke off and hid her face in her hands. She feared the horror of that moment would always be fresh in her mind.

"Please go on, Ms. Brinton."

Nickie lifted her head. "Miguel grabbed the phone and called the doctor." *And the look he shot me while*

*he punched out the numbers was the coldest, darkest
look I've ever seen.* "For the next little while everything was chaotic, but they finally got Katalin's temperature down again, thank God." Her voice shook
with emotion. *If anything had happened to that precious baby...*

"At that point what did you do?"

"I started to leave, and Marieli followed me to the
front door. She told me to get out of her house and
never come back. She warned me that if I ever went
near Miguel again, I'd regret the day I was born."
Miguel had remained in the background holding Katalin, icily uncommunicative in a way she'd never seen
him. She'd wanted to die.

"Did you start to date John Forrester after that incident?"

"No."

"Did you attempt to see or talk to Miguel Aldabe?"

"No. The next morning I resigned from my secretarial job without giving notice and withdrew from the
college."

"Why would you do that when you already had so
much invested in your career?"

"Because I would never deliberately hurt another
human being." Which was only a small portion of the
whole truth, but no one needed to know everything
that was in her heart. "If Marieli was in that much
pain because of my friendship with Miguel, I didn't
want to cause any more. I had no idea she harbored
that kind of anger toward me. She's always been a

quiet person and kept to herself. I never imagined she loathed me to that extent.

"Miguel married *her*, had a baby with *her*," Nickie blurted out, trying to disguise her own pain. "He's the most honorable man I've ever known, incapable of committing adultery. I'm Irene's friend and certainly never saw myself as a threat—not to Marieli, not to anyone."

"Did Miguel Aldabe try to talk to you or see you after that night?"

"No," she lied. The court didn't need to hear that Miguel had come by her house the next evening to castigate her in private over her negligence with Katalin. But Nickie had already left for Colorado, and when he'd discovered she wasn't home he'd demanded to know where she'd gone. Her parents refused to tell him or give him a phone number where she could be reached.

They remained adamant in their desire to protect Nickie from any more pain inflicted by Marieli or Miguel.

"Do you honestly expect this court to believe that after eighteen years of a relationship closer than most married couples', you haven't had any contact with him in the last eight months? That he didn't tell you he had filed for divorce?"

Nickie shook her head, wondering how she'd survived the questioning to this point. "No. I believed Marieli when she told me I'd regret it if I ever came near Miguel again. I decided the only way to convince her I posed no threat to their marriage was to go as far away as possible and never come back. Since that night, Miguel and I have not been in touch with each other. I had no idea he'd filed for divorce until my mother called me in Colorado Springs to tell me I'd been subpoenaed for this trial."

With a strange cold smile Aranburu said, "Your Honor, I have no further questions of this witness, but ask that she remain in the courtroom for recall."

The judge addressed Miguel's attorney. "Counselor? You wish to cross-examine?"

"No questions at this time, Your Honor."

"Mr. Helm?"

"No, Your Honor."

"The witness may step down."

Mr. Aranburu stood up. "If it please the bench, I wish to call Irene Aldabe to the stand."

CHAPTER THREE

NICKIE GOT unsteadily to her feet and made her way back to her place beside Mr. Helm. She could almost feel Miguel's dark gaze following her progress. She could imagine his expression of cold disdain and tried not to remember how he used to smile at her with warmth and lazy affection. She didn't dare acknowledge him. It would be too humiliating, too painful.

Her attorney patted her arm. "You get an A-plus for following my instructions to the letter, Nickie. You spoke with brevity and conviction, so I'm sure the judge knew you were telling the truth. This trial has backfired on Marieli Aldabe."

Not in her wildest fantasies could Nickie have conceived that a day like this would ever come. And as she heard her friend take the oath, Nickie knew Irene had to be thinking the same thing.

She'd missed their close friendship and frequent visits, but didn't realize how much until this very minute. She watched Irene perch on the edge of the seat, her body ramrod straight, her stoic expression a mask that Nickie knew hid pain and deep-seated fears.

Though of medium height, Irene was physically strong and lean like Miguel. They shared the typical Basque black-brown eyes and hair, and with their beautiful olive skin and engaging white smiles, Nickie found them both immensely attractive people.

Marieli's attorney launched immediately into his volley.

"Ms. Aldabe, is it true that you have not seen Ms. Brinton in the past eight months?"

"Yes."

"No communication?"

"None."

"After all the testimony that has been given concerning your friendship, I find it difficult to believe the two of you haven't written letters or called each other on the phone during that time. Why haven't you?"

"You know why, Mr. Aranburu."

"Answer the question, Ms. Aldabe," the judge prompted.

"Because Nickie couldn't take any more pain."

Irene's accurate assessment brought Nickie's head around and she eyed her mother, who commiserated with her in silence.

"What pain?"

"I arrived at Miguel's house a little while after Nickie had left, and let myself in. I could hear Marieli's sobs coming from the living room and I was shocked because I thought she and Miguel would be out all night.

"I went to ask what was wrong and saw her holding Katalin. When she caught sight of me, she started screaming, blaming me for putting the baby at risk because I'd let Nickie tend her. She said she and Miguel had come home early to find Nickie entertaining John Forrester. It was Nickie's fault, she claimed, that the baby's temperature had shot up again. Anything might have happened if she and Miguel hadn't arrived when they did.

"I suspected she was exaggerating, perhaps out of panic. But I realized she must have said the same things to Nickie who's conscientious to a fault and would *never* have let anything happen to the baby. Nickie must have been devastated. I didn't blame her for leaving and I respected her privacy too much to bother her. I knew that if she wanted to talk to me, she'd get in touch."

Nickie rubbed her forehead, where she felt a headache gathering force.

"Who asked you to baby-sit on the night of January third?"

"My brother."

"Did he explain why he wanted you to stay all night?"

"Yes. He said he and Marieli were going out for the evening and might not come home until morning. He wanted me to look after the baby because Katalin loved me and wouldn't be frightened if she woke up and found me there."

"Ms. Aldabe, knowing how much Dr. Aldabe trusted you, the court is surprised to hear that you let Nickie Brinton take over your duties. Isn't it because you knew how deeply she loved your brother that you let her baby-sit in your place? Anything to be close to him because she no longer worked at the library?"

"No, that's not true! When my brother asked me to baby-sit, he had no idea of the dilemma he'd put me in," Irene stated, jolting Nickie who started to fear the

worst. She shook her head to catch Irene's attention,
worried what she might say next.

"What dilemma was that, Ms. Aldabe?"

"I had important plans that I couldn't break, plans
that had been made six weeks before, but I didn't dare
disappoint my brother since he'd asked me a favor.
The fact is I—"

"No, Irene!" Nickie's voice resounded throughout
the courtroom.

The judge pounded his gavel. "Mr. Helm, please
advise your client that if there's another outburst I'll
have her restrained."

Jason Helm murmured gravely, "What's going on,
Nickie?"

"I—I'm not sure...." she whispered, lowering her
head. She was sick at heart, terrified that Irene might
sacrifice herself in a useless attempt to save Nickie's
reputation.

"Proceed, Ms. Aldabe."

"Miguel had no way of knowing that the night he
asked me to baby-sit was my wedding night."

After a terrible silence, pandemonium broke loose
in the courtroom, just as Nickie had feared. The judge
pounded his gavel, then stood to pound it with greater
force before sitting down again.

Compelled by an urge she could no longer resist,
Nickie darted a furtive glance at Miguel. In spite of the
gaping chasm between them, she was hungry for the
sight of his sun-bronzed aquiline features, his black
hair and lean, supple body. She experienced a shock
of sensuality every time she looked at him—she'd felt
this way since her early teens. Eight months' separa-

tion had only intensified those feelings. She could no more stifle her response to him than she could prevent an errant chill from racing down her spine.

Irene's admission had created havoc in the courtroom. While their parents huddled with other family members, conversing in Euskara, Miguel alone said nothing. He merely stared at his sister in disbelief.

Nickie knew what courage it had taken for Irene to defy generations of Basque tradition by marrying outside the community. And she knew the courage it took now to admit her guilty secret in front of the powerful Aldabe family. Unlike Miguel, the only son, who had remained true to filial commitment and married a Basque woman, Irene had chosen to break with her family to marry the man of her heart, a non-Basque. In marrying him, she not only risked losing her family's approval, she risked being disowned and disinherited.

Irene's gaze swerved to Nickie's just then, and they shared a private moment, exchanging a sympathy, an understanding that transcended words.

"Ms. Aldabe, do I need to remind you that perjury is a criminal offense?"

"Mr. Aranburu, I took an oath to tell the truth. The whole truth. That's what I've done. Fernando Arce and I were married by the Reverend Howard Welch at the Governor's Mansion in Carson City on January third at four o'clock in the afternoon. It's a matter of public record.

"Nickie Brinton stood as my witness, and Governor Andrew Cordell, along with his wife and son, stood up for my husband. He's one of the governor's bodyguards at the mansion. We planned to keep our marriage a secret until we felt my father's health had improved enough to handle the news.''

The courtroom was suddenly filled with the *irrintzi*, the strange high-pitched wail peculiar to the Basque people in times of intense emotion. The voice belonged to Begona Aldabe, Irene and Miguel's mother. The judge called repeatedly for order.

''Do you testify that your brother knew nothing about your marriage until this moment?'' Mr. Aranburu demanded.

''Nickie is the only person in this courtroom who knew about my marriage before today. As she testified earlier, Miguel is a very honorable man, and he expected me to uphold the family tradition by marrying Egoitz Darracq, a man to whom I've been promised since childhood.'' Irene paused to take a deep breath.

''But I could never marry a man my family picked out for me unless I loved him,'' she went on. ''I didn't love Egoitz and he didn't love me. Since I knew how much it would hurt both families when they found out the truth about my marriage, I chose to keep it a secret as long as possible.

''Immediately after the ceremony, I drove to my brother's home as if nothing had happened, to take care of Katalin. After he and Marieli left the house, Nickie surprised me by coming over and offering to relieve me so I could spend a few hours alone with my new husband.''

Suddenly Nickie felt Miguel's dark intent gaze on her, but for the life of her, she couldn't meet his eyes. And would never again....

"Nickie adores Katalin, and I knew the baby couldn't be in better hands. As Nickie testified, Katalin had been fussy and restless. But no one could have anticipated that her fever would go up like that.

"It was no one's fault, and it would have happened no matter who was looking after her. If there's anyone to blame, it's John Forrester who barged into Miguel's house under false pretenses and made things more complicated than they needed to be.

"What's so tragic is that Nickie was made to feel like a monster, and I for one wish to set the record straight. I also want to add that I intended to relieve Nickie before morning so Miguel and Marieli would never know she'd been there. But for some reason they came back early and discovered Nickie and John Forrester together. Mr. Forrester has done nothing but make a nuisance of himself ever since he met Nickie and—"

"That will be all, Ms. Aldabe." Marieli's attorney cut her off, his expression grim.

The judge then addressed Miguel's lawyer. "Ms. Henderson, do you wish to cross-examine this witness?"

"No, Your Honor."

"Mr. Helm?"

"No questions at this time, Your Honor."

"Then you may step down, Ms. Aldabe."

"The court calls Mr. John Forrester to the stand."

Jason Helm leaned toward Nickie. "Her testimony has weakened Marieli's case. You have a true friend in Irene Aldabe."

Nickie shivered. "I know. Poor Irene. She's done it now. I'm afraid her pain is just beginning."

"You could be right," he murmured compassionately as they watched Irene walk proudly from the stand to her seat amidst her relatives. Perocheguy Aldabe, Irene's father, turned his arthritic body away from his daughter and left the courtroom, leaning heavily on two canes. Begona sat straight in her seat staring rigidly ahead. Nickie wished she could alleviate everyone's suffering, but it was impossible.

"Mr. Forrester," Marieli's attorney began, "please tell the court where you live and your occupation."

"I rent an apartment near the campus of Reno City College, where I'm an assistant professor in the Basque-studies department."

"How long have you known Miguel Aldabe?"

"Miguel and I go back eight, nine years. We met when he came back to give a lecture at the University of Iowa."

"How would you characterize your relationship with him?"

"It's a professional one."

"In other words, you're not friends away from campus."

"No. Miguel Aldabe keeps to himself and only lets a select group of people into his life."

Not necessarily, Nickie wanted to shout. Miguel was everyone's favorite professor and had many eminent colleagues for friends throughout the world.

"Is he your equal or your superior at the college?"

"My superior."

"As a boss, what is he like to work for?"

"As I said, he's very professional, very civil."

"When did you first meet Nickie Brinton?"

"When I joined the staff three years ago."

"How did you meet her?"

"She was working in the Basque library and took several classes from me."

"What kind of student was she?"

"Very bright. Very intelligent. Gifted in the Basque language, which is rare."

"Did you ask Ms. Brinton to go out with you?"

"Yes."

"Do you often date your students?"

"Never. And Ms. Brinton wasn't technically my student at the time. Still, I've always been against professors getting involved with *any* student at the college—which is why it took me over two years before I finally broke my own rules and asked her out."

Nickie's eyes closed tightly. His "rules" hadn't stopped him from monopolizing her time at the library and conveniently showing up to walk her to class when he was the last person she wanted to see.

"Were you surprised when she turned you down for a date?"

"Disappointed would be a better word. From the beginning it was obvious to me that she was infatuated with Miguel Aldabe and he with her. Anyone who's around them will tell you the same thing."

"Objection!" Mr. Helm shouted. "Conjecture on the part of the witness."

"Sustained. Mr. Forrester, please stick to the facts."

"I'm only giving my opinion. The facts are, Nickie and Miguel Aldabe were constantly together, inseparable, if you will. I can understand why Marieli Aldabe would feel threatened, and after what I witnessed at the party on the Quinn ranch for Miguel Aldabe and his fiancée, my suspicions were verified. Despite his pending marriage to another woman, Miguel Aldabe was physically and emotionally involved with Nickie Brinton."

Nickie's heart started to thud with such intensity she could feel its beat in every part of her body.

"Please tell the court what you saw."

"Zackery Quinn knows how to throw a party. There was a barbecue, followed by dancing to an orchestra and all the champagne you could drink. Throughout the evening, I waited for an opportunity to get Nickie alone. She finally granted me one dance, then ran off and disappeared.

"The party broke up around two. I said good-night to Marieli, who was chatting with family members, and went looking for Nickie one last time, hoping I might be able to drive her home. Guests had been swimming in the pool on and off all evening and I thought maybe I'd find her there."

Nickie's skin started to prickle in apprehension.

"Though the lights had been turned off, there was a full moon and I discovered two people in the water."

Dear Lord. John had seen them in the pool. Nickie thought she was going to faint.

"Who were those people?"

"Miguel Aldabe and Nickie Brinton."

"You couldn't have mistaken either of them for anyone else?"

"I suppose I could have. They were at the deep end, away from me."

"Were they swimming?"

"No. From where I was standing, it looked like they were...embracing."

A wave of angry murmurs filled the courtroom. "Were they kissing?"

"I can't be positive. Miguel Aldabe's back was toward me and his head was lowered. I could see Nickie's arms around his neck."

With every word he uttered, Nickie felt a little sicker.

"What did you do?"

"I realized I had intruded on a very private moment and I left."

"Did you confront either of them later with this knowledge?"

"No. I had my career to think about."

"Why did you go to the Aldabe home on the night of January third?"

"To warn Nickie."

"What do you mean, warn her?"

"Marieli's aunt and uncle—her father's brother—are good friends of mine. She stayed with them whenever she and her parents visited Reno. The family talked freely about their hostility toward Nickie Brinton. They've considered her a serious threat to their daughter's marriage and have wanted her out of the picture for a long time.

"I still had strong feelings for Nickie and I didn't want to see her the subject of gossip and possible scandal. I figured Miguel Aldabe had some kind of hold on her, and I hoped that if she could ever get away from him and his possessiveness, maybe she'd come to see me in a different light. He guards her rather jealously."

It was hard for Nickie to believe anyone could be so vindictive. What John wasn't saying was that he was so jealous of Miguel he'd do anything to discredit him. Nickie hadn't thought she was capable of real hate, but right now her feelings bordered on it.

"How did you know she was at the Aldabe residence?"

"It was Friday, and I knew Nickie generally spent weekends at home with her family. I called her mother and told her I needed to talk to Nickie about something important. She assumed it had to do with her job at the college, so she told me Nickie was baby-sitting at the Aldabe home.

"When I heard that, I figured Nickie was digging herself in deeper, creating a situation Marieli's family would use against her. I decided to drop in without phoning ahead. For once I knew that neither Marieli nor Miguel Aldabe would be around and I thought it was a good time to surprise her. I hoped that if I told Nickie what I knew, she'd stop seeing me as the enemy. Maybe, in time, she'd agree to go out with me."

Nickie took a sharp breath.

John must be out of his mind.

"What happened when you arrived at the Aldabe home?"

"Exactly what Ms. Brinton testified. I told her that Miguel Aldabe had relieved her of her duties in the library because of family pressure, but she didn't believe me."

Nickie swallowed hard. Was *that* the reason Miguel had let her go? All this time she'd thought he'd found her work inferior. When he'd told her that another librarian had been hired and that he had finished his project and no longer required her help with his research, he'd been so aloof and unlike the Miguel she'd always known that she was shattered.

"Did you tell her what you'd seen in the swimming pool?"

"No. I was afraid I'd make a real enemy of Nickie if I did that. After all, what went on in the pool happened before Miguel married Marieli. I figured he was making the most of his opportunities before the wedding.

"As for Nickie, she was crazy about him, besotted, and I decided I'd better tread carefully. So I did the only other thing I could. I told her I'd fallen in love with her and begged her to give us a chance to get to know each other better. That's when the Aldabes walked in on us."

"I have no further questions of this witness."

As Nickie watched Mr. Aranburu go back to his table, Jason Helm whispered, "I'm putting you back on the stand. Get ready."

Nickie froze.

The judge said, "Ms. Henderson, do you wish to cross-examine?"

"I have no questions for the witness."

"Mr. Helm, do you wish to cross-examine?"

"No, Your Honor, but I'd like to recall Nickie Brinton."

With a feeling of dread, Nickie took her place on the stand, the bailiff reminding her that she was still under oath.

"Ms. Brinton," Jason Helm began, "the court has heard you testify that you have never slept with Miguel Aldabe in your eighteen-year association with him. You've testified that you have always looked upon him as a brother. Keeping that in mind, would you please tell the court if you were the woman in the swimming pool with Miguel Aldabe the night Zackery Quinn gave a party for the engaged couple."

Her body went hot, then cold. "Yes. I was the woman."

"Tell us what happened in the swimming pool on the night Mr. Forrester testified that he thought he saw you and Miguel Aldabe embracing. Were you, in fact, embracing?"

"No."

"Did you two purposely plan to meet there because you knew Marieli Aldabe was occupied elsewhere?"

"No."

"Tell the court what really happened that night. Take all the time you need," he said kindly.

"Because of a term paper that was due the next day, I thanked Zack—Mr. Quinn—for the invitation, but told him I wouldn't be able to come to the party. He refused to take no for an answer and insisted on flying me to the ranch no matter how late the hour. He invited me, along with several other guests, to stay overnight. He's a very persuasive man and I finally agreed to come. I must have arrived there around eleven.

"The party was well under way. I talked to Marieli and Miguel for a few minutes and congratulated them, then I spent time chatting with Irene and a few of her cousins. John Forrester and I danced one dance. By then, Randy Cordell, Mr. Quinn's nephew, saw me and asked me to join him and some of his friends for a midnight horseback ride.

"I love to ride, so I went with them. We were gone a couple of hours. Afterward we went swimming. Before I knew it, Mr. Quinn and Miguel had joined us for a water fight. Pretty soon, everyone was exhausted and left the pool.

"As I started to climb out of the deep end, Miguel held me back because he said he wanted to talk to me for a minute. I told him I was tired, but he said it wouldn't take long."

"What did he want to say to you?"

Nickie took a fortifying breath. "He told me that I should be careful not to encourage Randy, who, he said, had an enormous crush on me. It seems he and Mr. Quinn had overheard Randy asking me to come back to the ranch the following weekend for a campout. Both men were worried that Randy, who'd lost his mother and was looking for affection, would get hurt if he spent any more time with me.

"I resented his comments. I was well aware that Randy was only seventeen and very vulnerable, and I told Miguel I could handle Randy without hurting him. I reminded Miguel that he was Irene's brother, not mine.

"Miguel laughed and asked me to forgive him, saying he'd probably come on too strong. But I was irritated with him and Mr. Quinn for underestimating me. I told him I wouldn't forgive him and I tried to get away. He refused to take me seriously and dunked me in the water. I should explain that he's always teased Irene and me from the time we were all kids. Since I couldn't touch bottom, I instinctively grabbed on to him."

"Did you notice Mr. Forrester in the background?"

"No." She hadn't been aware of anything but the feel of Miguel's hands on her shoulders, the closeness of their bodies. She'd wanted him so badly. "When Miguel let me up for air, he asked me again if I'd forgiven him. I finally said yes, and he told me he hoped his marriage to Marieli wouldn't prevent us from remaining good friends. Then he thanked me for coming to the party, kissed my forehead and let me go."

"Does Miguel Aldabe have a habit of kissing you in this manner?"

"No." Her voice shook. "That was the one and only kiss he has ever given me."

And therein lay her sin. She'd wanted much more from him than the one chaste kiss he'd bestowed on her out of brotherly affection.

"I have no further questions."

The judge lifted his head. "Does either counsel wish to cross-examine?" Both responded in the negative, and the judge told Nickie she could step down. "The court will take a five-minute recess."

The second he pounded the gavel, the room exploded in a cacophony of voices. The Echevarria and

Aldabe families both surrounded Marieli and escorted her from the room. But Nickie's attention focused on Irene, whose husband had suddenly appeared out of nowhere. Nickie sighed in relief when she saw him slip a comforting arm around her waist. Irene had probably never felt so alone in her life.

Against her will, Nickie's gaze found Miguel, who sat at the table conversing with his attorney. The revelation that he'd fired Nickie because of pressure from the Echevarria family put a whole new light on things. To some extent, it explained why he'd seemed so distant and remote, almost a stranger.

She was still reeling from the impact of this new understanding when Zackery Quinn and his wife, Alex, stepped back into the courtroom. The second Miguel saw them, he sprang from his seat and in a few long strides reached his best friend. They gave each other a fierce hug, then he embraced Alex.

Rarely did Miguel show affection in public. This uncharacteristic reaction could only mean his emotions lurked close to the surface.

Despite everything, she couldn't take her eyes off Miguel. He was tall for a Basque, taller even than Zackery Quinn, who had to be a good six feet. In his conservative suit of charcoal gray with a white shirt and dark tie, Miguel possessed an air of reserved sophistication. She thought he completely looked the part of the erudite professor—Dr. Aldabe whose enviable publishing credits in academic circles had given him worldwide acclaim.

But beneath that civilized veneer stood a broad-shouldered man whose powerfully muscled body was capable of extraordinary endurance and strength.

On one of her visits to Irun, Nickie had watched him play pelota, the Basque national game. Miguel's countrymen either played it with a *chistera,* a wicker glove in a court with four walls, or bare-handed in a court with only one wall.

The object was to slam the ball into the opposing side's area with such speed and accuracy as to stay in bounds but be unreturnable. Bare-handed, Miguel delivered the ball with such momentum Nickie literally couldn't see it in flight. Before the game was over, two opponents had suffered broken wrists trying to return his volley.

The kind of skill and stamina required for such a feat staggered Nickie. She viewed Miguel with even greater awe than before. It made perfect sense that he could outrace any bikers along the Flume Trail at Lake Tahoe's northeast edge. The high altitude alone defeated most people, but not Miguel, who thrived in a mountain atmosphere.

Back in the Pyrenees, she'd often watched him run up perilously steep slopes and jump mountain ledges five to ten feet apart without the slightest hesitation. Equally at home on a horse, he was the only man she knew who could match Zackery Quinn's mastery in the saddle.

Despite the anger she knew he felt toward her, despite eight months' separation and her deliberate attempt to date as many other men as possible, she couldn't escape Miguel Aldabe's image. It had always managed to insinuate itself and dominate her thoughts, her feelings. As a result, she'd found it impossible to form a relationship with even the most attractive and ardent admirer.

Nickie frowned at the implication and looked away. As soon as the trial was over, she intended to take a late-afternoon or evening flight back to Denver. Her family would be upset, but she couldn't think beyond her own desperate need to break completely with the past and find a new life.

Thanks to the advice of her counselor at the college, she had the necessary background in French to go on for a Master's degree in Arabic. From there she could pursue a Ph.D. in anthropology with an emphasis in Egyptology, as the counselor had suggested, and get involved in a new research project.

Her parents were right. She'd be a fool to throw away all those years of education. Just because Basque studies now had to be ruled out didn't mean her academic career had to come to an end.

If she worked in her uncle's store until the end of the year she could earn enough money to repay the attorney's fee and manage her tuition. Then she could start school in January. Most of the colleges in Colorado were on the semester system. She'd look into it as soon as she got back.

Working for her uncle provided her with an income, but it couldn't prevent her from thinking about Miguel. If studying would help dull the pain and erase all those memories, she would immerse herself in a new discipline—for as long as it took!

CHAPTER FOUR

"ALL RISE," the bailiff called out.

The judge entered the room and took his seat. "Mr. Aranburu, you may make your closing remarks."

"Thank you, Your Honor." He took his place and looked around the courtroom, eyes narrowed, staring deliberately at Nickie. If her father hadn't clasped her hand, Nickie didn't know how she would have survived the moment.

"Your Honor, from the time that Miguel Aldabe first began visiting my client Marieli Echevarria Aldabe in Irun, she has been a victim of his cruel and unconscionable insensitivity. The couple was affianced from birth, and he and his family made repeated trips to the Pyrenees to bring them together. Like every good Basque daughter, she awaited his visits with expectation and longing.

"When they both reached twenty-one, it was understood they would marry. To Marieli's humiliation, to her family's shame, he didn't come to Irun that summer as anticipated. Instead, he showed up five months later with his friend, Zackery Quinn. He gave no word of explanation or apology and made no mention of marriage.

"When my client confronted him, he told her he would not marry until he had established his professional career. When she reasoned that they could marry immediately and live in San Sebastian while he attended the university there, he refused to entertain her ideas because he intended to pursue his studies in the United States. He told her he wouldn't make her his wife until he could support a family, which is ludicrous, considering the vast Aldabe wealth.

"Year after year Marieli waited to say her vows with Miguel Aldabe. Year after year she suffered torment as he periodically dropped in for short visits, only to leave again with no firm commitment. Year after year she watched her friends marry and have children while her fiancé followed his own agenda in a country thousands of miles away.

"She assumed that after eight years of academic pursuit he would finally come to claim her. In time he did return, but he wasn't alone. Oh, no. This time, he brought another woman, Nickie Brinton. This time, instead of traveling at will with a male companion, he barely took the time to say hello to his fiancée before disappearing for ten days with Ms. Brinton, ostensibly to do research."

Nickie squeezed her father's hand in a death grip.

"At that point my client had no choice but to come to the United States and live with relatives in Reno, where she could be near him until such time as he finally condescended to marry her and honor their contract.

"Ms. Brinton's conduct leaves no question in anyone's mind. From the very beginning, her willful, persistent and intimate association with Miguel Aldabe has brought about an alienation of affection that has resulted in divorce—a divorce my client did not want or seek, a divorce that has broken a sacred trust between two honorable families.

"Therefore, Your Honor, because from the beginning Miguel Aldabe has shown a flagrant disregard for the prenuptial agreement, because he carried on an eighteen-year relationship with Nickie Brinton, ignoring his dutiful fiancée and wife's tenderest feelings, and because he forced her to lose precious years of wedded bliss that can never be recaptured, my client begs the court to award her custody of her daughter, Katalin. She is also requesting ten million dollars in punitive damages, plus the home on Lake Tahoe where she has lived throughout their short marriage—the only home her daughter has known—as fair and just compensation."

Mr. Aranburu flashed Nickie a final venomous glance and sat down. Though he repulsed her, the powerful case he had just presented brought out Nickie's compassionate instincts. When she put herself in Marieli's place, she could understand why the other woman had become embittered and desperate enough to try almost anything to win Miguel's affection.

To wait all your life for the man you loved, only to have it end like this must be unbearable.

If Miguel had treated Marieli to the same kind of cold angry contempt he'd shown Nickie that last night at his house, then Nickie felt sorry for Marieli. She'd suffered, and it was her suffering that had caused her to charge Miguel with adultery. Nickie could even forgive Marieli for naming her as the other woman, a reaction she wouldn't have thought possible when her mother first called to give her the bad news.

"Ms. Henderson? You may proceed with your final summation."

"Thank you, Your Honor." Miguel's attorney got up from the table and addressed the court. "Opposing counsel has treated this court to a long history of matters that do not have any bearing on this divorce suit. My client has testified that he never slept with Nickie Brinton, and she has testified to the same.

"It has been firmly established that Nickie Brinton is Irene Aldabe's closest friend, which explains the long-standing friendship between the three of them. In spite of their eighteen-year association, opposing counsel has failed to produce one single solitary piece of concrete evidence to prove that my client has ever engaged in an adulterous relationship with Nickie Brinton. The reason is that there *was* no affair. Their regard for each other has been established as that of brother and sister.

"May I also point out that there has been no evidence brought forth in this trial to suggest that my client has ever had a sexual relationship with any woman other than his wife. It is this counsel's opinion that he has led a remarkably chaste existence and has displayed a steadfast faithfulness toward his fiancée.

"He can't be blamed for wanting to establish his career first, not when she testified that she had no interest in his academic pursuits. Because he knew how she felt, he refused to put her through years of neglect while he immersed himself in his studies.

"When my client became the director of Basque studies, he married Marieli Echevarria in good faith. But since that time, irreconcilable differences— brought out in his testimony—have led my client to seek a divorce, namely because of their incompatibility, both mental and emotional.

"The charges of adultery continued long after my client fired Ms. Brinton from the library and released her from her work on his project. After she dropped out of the college, he had no contact with her. He can do nothing about his wife's accusations, which she continues to throw at him unceasingly despite the fact that Ms. Brinton left the state eight months ago and has only come back for the trial.

"As opposing counsel has pointed out, the Basque department's Ph.D. program here in Reno is unique. Thus, in absenting herself from this campus, Ms. Brinton has unselfishly jeopardized her own academic career to show good faith.

"In suing for divorce, my client is willing to give Marieli Aldabe the ten-million-dollar settlement. He is also willing to deed her the lakefront house and property as drawn up in the prenuptial agreement, which will settle a long-standing dispute between the two families. What my client asks for is full and reasonable visitation rights with their daughter, Katalin.

"My client has been more than generous in the financial settlement. He wishes Marieli Aldabe well and hopes that despite their irreconcilable differences they can find an amicable way to work out Katalin's future.''

When she'd finished speaking, a buzz of voices filled the courtroom, prompting the judge to pound his gavel to restore order. Nickie's heart raced with anxiety as she awaited his final verdict.

He sat forward to address the court. ''The plaintiff, Miguel Aldabe, brings this proceeding to obtain a divorce from his wife, alleging incompatibility. The defendant, Marieli Aldabe, by counterclaim, alleges cruel misconduct on his part.

''The alleged misconduct consists in persistent close association with a young woman, Nickie Brinton. Counsel for Mrs. Aldabe has provided many instances of documented times and places when both parties were together, and at periods alone together, over an eighteen-year period. However, the modern conception of relations between the sexes does not frown on ordinary association between a married man and another woman within the bounds of friendship alone.

''A determination as to whether an association or conduct of one spouse with a person of the opposite sex, short of adultery, constitutes legal cruelty, must rest almost entirely upon the individual facts of each case.

''In this case, Dr. Aldabe has denied the charge of adultery, and so has Ms. Brinton. When Mrs. Aldabe expressed her unhappiness about his relationship with Ms. Brinton, her husband discharged Ms. Brinton from her library job and his project at the college. When Mrs. Aldabe threatened Ms. Brinton the night she was baby-sitting, Ms. Brinton left the state altogether without finishing her graduate degree. Such action has jeopardized her career in her chosen field. These actions, on the part of both the plaintiff and Ms. Brinton, rule out legal cruelty.

"The surface evidence and testimony presented in this case shows that the relationship between Dr. Aldabe and Ms. Brinton was more like that of brother and sister, a relationship simply deepened by Ms. Brinton's close association with his sister, and by both parties' similar educational backgrounds and academic interests at one of the only colleges in the Western world where they might pursue their careers to the fullest extent.

"In this instance the court rules that no proof exists of actual adultery."

"We won, Nickie," Jason Helm whispered, and patted her arm, but Nickie was still reacting to the fact that Miguel's marriage had been so tragic.

"In the matter of their daughter, Katalin, custody is awarded to the mother, with full and reasonable visitation rights given to the father. Counsels will work out details of visitation, holidays, et cetera."

Nickie expelled her breath slowly, thankful the judge had allowed Miguel full visitation rights. She knew how much he adored the baby. When he was around Katalin, he was almost a different person, carefree and open in his love, without the brooding that sometimes surrounded him.

"After a lengthy study of the assets of the plaintiff," the judge continued, "which include other properties, business investments, savings in stocks and bonds, it is the opinion of this court that the defendant's plea for relief exceeds what the court deems a fair and equitable settlement to compensate her and her daughter.

"Therefore the court awards the defendant a five-million-dollar settlement, plus the Lake Tahoe house and property.

"With no other business before the court, divorce is granted, and court is adjourned." He pounded his gavel, then Nickie heard him call both attorneys to the bench and ask who would prepare the order. After that, the noise in the courtroom became deafening.

Her mother hugged her first. Then her father embraced her with fierce affection, almost knocking the wind out of her. "It's over," he said hoarsely, "and you can put this behind you."

"Amen," chimed her attorney. But Nickie suspected her torment was just beginning. She pulled away from her father.

"Thank you, Mr. Helm. I couldn't have handled this without you."

"She's right," her mother said. "You were wonderful."

"That's always nice to hear. Now I hope you'll forgive me, but I've got to get back to the office to prepare for another trial in the morning."

Nickie's father grabbed her arm. "We'll leave with you."

With the men on either side, escorting like an honor guard, they walked up the aisle. Nickie stared straight ahead and tried to ignore the icy contempt and hurtful glares of Begona Aldabe and the dozens of Aldabe and Echevarria relatives who parted to let them through, then huddled in groups no doubt to cast more aspersions on the woman they would always refer to as the adulteress.

Just before she reached the back door she saw Irene and Fernando out of the corner of her eye. Her friend mouthed the words "I'll call you," and Nickie nodded to her before leaving the courtroom. She couldn't get out of there, out of Reno, fast enough.

"NICKIE!"

The familiar female voice brought Nickie's head around, and she looked for Irene over the heads of the other passengers getting ready to board the plane.

The minute she saw her friend's face, Nickie stepped out of line and ran toward her.

"Thank heaven you haven't left yet," Irene cried softly as they threw their arms around each other. The next thing Nickie knew, they were both in tears, too full of emotion to speak.

Recovering first, Nickie murmured, "I'll never be able to thank you for what you did for me today. I hope you won't live to regret it."

"Don't be ridiculous," Irene said, wiping her eyes. "Let's face it, the trial was ghastly for everyone. I know you don't ever want to talk or think about it again. Neither do I, but I couldn't let you get away without saying goodbye."

Swallowing a sob, Nickie said, "I would have phoned you, but I didn't know where to reach you and didn't dare call your parents. I waited for your call as long as I could, but I'm on standby, so I had to be at the airport as soon as possible." The best she'd been able to get was a flight to Salt Lake City. Her uncle was going to meet her there and drive her back to Colorado Springs.

"I know. When I phoned the house your brother told me you'd just left for the airport with your parents. I don't blame you for wanting to escape but Nickie—" Irene's voice trembled "—I've missed you. There's so much I have to tell you."

Nickie's response was to hug her friend harder. "Give me a phone number where I can reach you and I'll call you as soon as I get to my aunt and uncle's. I've got to talk to you, too, or I think I'll go crazy."

"That's how I've felt ever since you left eight months ago." She reached into her purse for a piece of paper and they exchanged phone numbers and addresses. "I've rented an apartment in Carson City. It's near the Governor's Mansion. Fernando spends as much time with me as he can. I've got a job at a travel agency and I've written down that number, too. You can call me there anytime."

"Mom and Dad told me about it." Nickie brushed the tears from her cheeks. "How are things going?"

"All right, but I have to be honest. Without you around, there's been a void."

The tears started again. "I know what you mean—I feel the same way. How's Fernando?"

"He's wonderful. After what went on in the courtroom today, I know more than ever that I did the right thing in marrying him. I don't even care if my family never speaks to me again because of it. I won't let them do to me what they did to Miguel. Anyone could see he and Marieli are a total mismatch."

"Until Mom called and told me about the trial, I had no idea they weren't getting along."

"Miguel hides everything so well most people don't have a clue what goes on inside him. I hate the whole cruel insane tradition of arranged marriages that ruin people's lives before they've even started to live. I blame my father and mother for putting unbearable pressure on Miguel from the minute he took his first breath. I blame Marieli's parents for expecting her to marry a man they chose for her.

"It's all because of money and land and power. It's so wrong, Nickie. If I'd been forced to marry Egoitz, we would have ended up exactly like Marieli and Miguel."

"How do you think Egoitz is going to take it when he hears you're already married?"

"His parents will never speak to mine again. As for him, if he's honest he'll be out of his mind with joy. He never loved me and probably dreaded our marriage as much as I did. But he's a lot like Miguel. He honors tradition and keeps everything to himself. I'm praying there's someone else he already cares for. What happened to my brother and Marieli should never happen to another human being."

Nickie gave a despairing sigh.

"I don't blame Marieli for feeling hurt and betrayed because Miguel obviously never loved her. But how could she have been this cruel to him—to all of us? Why? He was willing to give her the house, the money, everything she wanted, without going through an ugly trial. It doesn't make sense to me. She almost sounds...unbalanced."

"I know," Irene muttered. "Maybe she is. Maybe her unfulfilled expectations drove her over the edge. I guess we'll never really know."

Nickie moaned. "She's been so unhappy, and all because of me."

"That's absurd, Nickie. You were just a convenient scapegoat for her pain."

Nickie wished she shared Irene's practical outlook on life. "Thank heaven little Katalin is too young to know what's going on. I've missed holding her. She's probably grown so much I wouldn't recognize her."

"She'll be walking on her own pretty soon." Irene rummaged for her wallet and pulled out a snapshot. "Here—this is for you. I took it last week."

The dark curly-haired cherub with the shining black eyes and hair was standing on unsteady legs, clutching the edge of the coffee table in Miguel's living room.

Nickie felt a tug at her heart. "She's adorable, isn't she?"

"I hope ours will be as cute."

"*What?*" Nickie's head jerked back. "Are you telling me you're—"

"Pregnant!" Irene had stars in her eyes. "I'm due in March."

"Oh, Irene," Nickie cried, hugging her friend once more. "I'm so happy for you. Is Fernando ecstatic?"

At her question, Irene pulled away. "I haven't told him yet."

"Why?"

"He's been so upset because we haven't been able to tell anyone about our marriage. I was afraid if I told him about the baby, he wouldn't be able to keep it to himself."

"Well, after today everyone in Carson City knows you're Mrs. Fernando Arce, so I guess you can tell him now that he's going to be a father."

Irene blushed. "Yes, you're right." When the final boarding was announced, she reached out to grab Nickie's arm. "Promise me you'll call the minute you get to Colorado Springs. I haven't begun to tell you everything."

"You know I will." They hugged one last time. "I've got to go. Promise me you'll take care of yourself. I can't wait to hold your baby."

"If it's a girl, I'm naming her after you."

"You shouldn't have told me that. Now I'll cry all the way to Colorado. Thank you for this." She held up Katalin's picture before hurrying through the door to the gangway. *It was all she had left of Miguel.*

"DR. ALDABE?"

"Yes?" Miguel said without looking up from his work, hoping his secretary wasn't bringing him any more cheery Christmas cards or messages. He couldn't stand the thought of it.

"Mr. Quinn is here to see you."

He lifted his head. "Send him in, Cora." Miguel shoved himself away from the desk and reached the door of his office in a few long strides. "You're a sight for sore eyes," he muttered, clapping Zack on the shoulder. "Come on in and sit down."

"I flew in this morning for the Cattlemen's convention. It just broke up and I decided to deliver Alex's invitation in person. She wants you to come to dinner at the ranch tonight. Little Sean misses his godfather." Miguel half smiled, missing Katalin and envying Zack his son. "My instructions are to fly you back with me, no ifs, ands or buts. She says you've hibernated long enough in these hallowed halls, and I agree with her."

"Zack, you know there's nothing I'd like better," Miguel said as he perched on the edge of his desk. "But it's the last day of finals and I'm swamped. By the time I finish the paperwork, it could be close to midnight."

"You look like hell. When was the last time you had any sleep?"

"I've forgotten, but it doesn't matter. Tomorrow I'm flying to Europe to finish some research I need for my book. I won't be able to spend the Christmas holidays with you and Alex, much as I'd like to. My publisher has given me until January fifteenth. Even working round the clock, I don't know how I'll meet the deadline.

"My personal life has disrupted my routine for too long, and unfortunately there's only one person who was in on my project from the beginning who'd be able to help me. But she isn't available." His voice shook with long-suppressed emotion.

"You mean Nickie." Zack seized the opportunity. "I've been wondering how long it would take before you were ready to talk about her."

Miguel felt as if he'd just been kicked in the stomach. He flung himself into his chair. "I'm afraid that's one subject better left alone."

"You brought it up, I didn't," Zack said brusquely. "Now I'm going to give you a piece of your own advice. It's the same thing you told me when I'd all but given up hope of winning Alex around. You said don't let her get away. Do whatever you have to do to convince her that neither of your lives is worth living without the other." After a brief pause, he added, "I took your advice and it's made me the happiest man on earth."

Miguel reached for his pipe and lit it. "The circumstances don't compare, Zack."

"They never do. That's the hell of it, and the challenge."

Unable to remain seated, Miguel got up from the chair and stood by the window, staring blindly into space. "She testified that she loved me like a brother," he said, his voice grating. He wheeled around. *"A brother!"*

"Miguel, you and Marieli lived a lie for years. It's entirely possible Nickie's been lying, too, but you'll never know the truth unless you confront her in person."

"I've brought enough pain into her life."

"Then end it. You're the only one who can. Surely at this point you're not afraid of the gossip."

"About me?" His harsh laugh reverberated within the small office. "Hardly. I've been crucified a hundred times over."

"So has she. What's the difference?"

"She's gone, Zack. She's been living another life in Colorado for the past eleven months."

"Have you considered the possibility that she's been miserable, too? That she's just been existing, surviving from one day to the next—"

"It's all I've been able to think about," Miguel muttered. He felt a surge of relief at saying the words aloud, in all their naked honesty. "Why do you think I can't get anything accomplished, why I can't even think?" he exploded. "She infiltrated my life years ago. It's like she's always been a part of me, a part of my soul. Without her I'm only half there. I can hardly function anymore."

"Well, what do you know? Miguel Aldabe has finally admitted he's as vulnerable as the next guy."

He darted Zack a wounded glance. "Did you think I wasn't?"

"Oh, no. I'm very much aware how human you are. I'm just relieved to hear you admit it. Some of those Basque genes must be for stubbornness. Reminds me of a couple of my prize steers."

A slow smile broke the corner of Miguel's mouth. "Have I ever told you what a great friend you are and always have been to me?"

Zack nodded. "Yes, but not in so many words. The divorce has changed you almost beyond recognition—and that's the first positive thing to happen to you in years." On a more sober note he said, "It's too bad you couldn't have gone after her as soon as the trial was over."

After a pause Miguel said, "She's needed time, Zack, and I've had the property and adoption legalities to deal with. Thank God that's all over."

"How does it feel to know you're free? To be able to take charge of your own destiny?"

Miguel's response was a long time in coming. "I don't have an answer to that yet."

"But you're going to find out!" Zack insisted with an intensity that spoke to Miguel's soul. They stared hard at each other for a long moment.

"I *have* to find out," Miguel admitted in a savage whisper, "otherwise I'll die without ever knowing what it was like to really be alive."

CHAPTER FIVE

AN ICY GUST OF WIND entered the Timberhaus with Miguel. He shut the door and brushed the snow from his parka. It was almost seven. A few more minutes and the store would be closed for the night.

After stamping more snow from his boots on a throw rug, he looked around until he caught sight of her honey blond hair over in the far corner. He didn't have to be next to her to know how sweet she smelled, like an alpine meadow alive with spring flowers.

Nickie.

He felt a stab of jealousy when he noticed she was helping two male skiers who appeared to be more interested in her than in the bibs she was showing them.

Aware she hadn't noticed his arrival yet, Miguel moved behind a goggle display on one of the counters and waited for the skiers to leave. After five minutes they made their purchases but still hung around her, slowly pulling on their gloves and woolen ski masks, chatting, joking, laughing. They were obviously interested in Nickie and trying to impress her, ignoring the fact that it was past closing time.

Miguel understood the attraction better than any man. It would be so easy to toss both of them out into the blizzard on their grinning raccoon faces and not feel the slightest remorse.

Even as a little girl she glowed with an inner light that radiated to her skin, her eyes, her silky hair. But it was her laughing white smile that first captivated his heart and made him feel a need, almost an obligation to protect her, to watch over her. Then, suddenly one day, without warning, his sunny fair-haired cherub turned into a breathtaking woman whose curves took on a voluptuousness he hadn't been prepared for.

The skiers couldn't take their eyes off her. Neither could he. She wore beige pants and a Scandinavian sweater designed in brown, tan and white; the colors emphasized the sheen of her hair and healthy complexion. What he'd missed most were her velvety brown eyes, dark as poppy throats.

Like a lighted candle in a dark room, she drew him to her generous warmth and he asked no more of life than to be allowed to bask in that glow until the end of his days. He *had* to see her face-to-face. Had to hear her low clear voice, saying words meant for him alone.

Just as his impatience reached its peak, the two skiers departed with the cocky assertion that they'd be back the next day to take her to lunch. Miguel had to suppress the urge to tell them they could forget it. She wouldn't be living in Colorado after tonight. Not if he had anything to do with it.

While she locked the front door he moved toward her. "*Egunon,* Nickie."

She gasped, then spun around.

He'd wanted the element of surprise on his side so he could glimpse her first unguarded reaction to seeing him again. But he hadn't expected the color to drain from her face. Nor did he like the look of fear mingled with the pain he saw in her eyes before they avoided his. It twisted something deep in his gut. Most of all, the bewitching smile he'd always associated with her was nowhere in evidence.

"I didn't mean to startle you," he told her gently. "I was waiting until you'd finished with your other customers."

"W-when did you come in?"

"A few minutes ago."

After a tense silence she cried, "This has to do with Irene, doesn't it? Did she lose the baby, or has something happened to Fernando? She's always been afraid he'd be hurt in the line of du—"

"All three of them are fine," he said emphatically, wanting to calm her anxiety.

But his pronouncement seemed to bring her up short. After another uncomfortable silence she said, "Then I don't understand why you're here."

He sucked in a breath. "You mean you can't conceive of my wanting to talk to you unless something catastrophic has happened to Irene?" he demanded, sounding more harsh than he'd intended.

"After being accused of adultery, I don't know how you could ask me that question." Her voice trembled with unconcealed distress. "I think you'd better leave, Miguel. I—if anyone knew you were here—" she broke off. With an abruptness that devastated him, she moved to the counter, apparently to take care of any unfinished business so she could leave for the night.

Miguel followed at a slower pace. In the whole of their lives she'd never put up a defensive shield against him before. He feared he might not be able to breach it.

"Your parents know why I'm here because I had a long talk with them before I left Nevada. Your aunt and uncle know because I phoned their house inquiring about you before I drove over here. If by anyone you mean Marieli, then you're being apprehensive for no good reason. The day after our divorce, she and Egoitz were married at the lake house. Zack and I witnessed their private ceremony."

Nickie had started counting the money in the till, but at that revelation her hands shook so badly she knocked the bills onto the floor and had to hunt for them.

Miguel understood that she didn't want his help, that she needed a moment to compose herself. There was so much Nickie didn't know about everything that had happened. So much he needed to tell her.

Slowly her head came up and she put the money on the counter without looking at it. "Marieli is *married?*" Her voice came out in a squeak. "To Egoitz? Irene's fiancé?"

"Bai," he responded in Euskara. "It turns out they've been lovers since Marieli was sixteen."

Nickie looked shocked. "And he never let on to Irene?"

"He couldn't tell her."

She shook her head. "I can't take it in. But you and Marieli had a baby!"

His expression tightened. "No, Nickie. We never slept together. Katalin is Egoitz's daughter."

For a moment Nickie seemed to be on the verge of fainting. She clutched the counter until her fingers lost color. Miguel's first instinct was to put his arms around her and never let her go, but from the dazed expression in her eyes he knew she'd reject any such overture.

"You're lying!" Her voice throbbed with emotion. "Katalin has your hair and coloring. The shape of her limbs a-and her hands."

So she is aware of my physical appearance. He supposed it was something.... "I've often been told that Egoitz and I share a superficial resemblance, and we're both Basque, after all. No, Nickie. Katalin is his child. If you need proof I can show you the printout of the DNA tests. Marieli and Egoitz are Katalin's parents."

"*DNA tests?*"

"Egoitz has loved Marieli for too long without being able to live with her. He went a little crazy when she told him she was pregnant with their child. In all the years they've been together, she had never conceived, and it was an ironic twist of fate that she suddenly became pregnant after marrying me. It complicated our plans in ways you can't possibly imagine, and for a while Marieli feared that until we could offer him absolute proof of paternity, she'd lose Egoitz."

Nickie stared at Miguel like an injured doe he'd once come across in the mountains, a creature who understood pain and nothing else. In a brittle voice she said, "All these years none of you has ever let on. You've betrayed everyone—Irene most of all."

"That's right," he said. "We've been pawns in a game orchestrated by our families. As you once remarked to me, we Basques possess a stoic quality. In Marieli's and Egoitz's case, as well as mine, it's worked to our advantage. We've been able to survive an impossible situation, one that was forced on us."

"How long ago did the three of you plan this... deception?" Her question came out in jerky breaths.

"On one of my visits to Irun in my late teens, Marieli asked me to go for a walk with her. She took me to a spot where Egoitz was waiting. What they told me made me happier than you could possibly imagine, because I had no interest in her beyond friendship. And it made me doubly happy for Irene, because down the road she would be spared a loveless marriage, too."

"Down the road...." Nickie let out an angry laugh.

"Hear me out, Nickie. During that visit the three of us made a pact. We agreed that if there was any way to get out of our marriages without dishonoring the families, we'd find it. Since I was a year older than Egoitz and would be expected to marry first, I promised to put off the actual ceremony to Marieli as long as possible to give all of us time to come up with a different solution." He could sense Nickie's mind working furiously.

"So that's why she never accompanied you and me on any of our trips or showed the slightest interest in your work? Because she wanted to be with Egoitz?"

He nodded.

"But during the trial, Marieli's attorney said that before we went to the Caucasus, you and she had a bitter argument because you wouldn't let her come with us!"

Miguel could see this was going to take time.

"It was all part of the deception," he began. "Marieli learned to be a superb actress, and she always pretended to be the victim while her parents attacked me. They made it very obvious that they were suspicious of all my dealings with you. They wanted to punish me—and you."

"By getting me fired from my job? Charging me with adultery when she knew I was innocent?" Nickie cried out in agony. "How could she do that? How could she let it go that far? Think of all the people she hurt!"

"You're blaming the wrong person, Nickie. Marieli's parents were the ones responsible for all the pain inflicted on you. They even hired someone to keep tabs on us in Turkey and Georgia."

"Why would they do that?" she demanded, aghast.

The way Nickie was looking at him made Miguel shudder. "Because I kept postponing our marriage," he told her baldly. "They decided there must be another woman involved. They needed someone to blame. So they picked you as their target—the only real innocent in this whole mess."

After a tension-filled silence, she asked, "Was it part of your plan to take Irene with you every time you traveled to the Pyrenees?"

"Ez," he denied swiftly. "My parents sent her along so she could get better acquainted with Egoitz and become comfortable with him."

Nickie's eyes narrowed. "So everyone had a motive." Disappointment was mirrored in her eyes. "Everyone played a part. Except for Irene."

"Yes," he conceded grimly. "I agreed to take the blame for any problems because it didn't matter what the families thought about me. I used the demands of my career as the excuse for not wanting Marieli with me and delaying the wedding plans. You're as aware as anyone that in a traditional Basque home the man stands at the head, and I knew her parents would be forced to abide by my decision as to when we'd marry, no matter how furious they were with me."

Nickie's expression darkened. He could feel her disbelief and confusion. She felt betrayed, and who could blame her? Years of lies lay waiting to be uncovered. But it was the way the light faded from her eyes, making them dull and lifeless, that pierced his heart.

"Do you hate me so much for deceiving you?" His voice sounded strange even to him.

She lowered her head and started putting the money into a bag. "Of course not. Your business has always been your own affair. As I testified in court, I'm Irene's friend and I have no right to judge. It has nothing to do with me." She spoke in remote tones, freezing him out. "Just tell me one thing ..."

She paused. "After the trial, Irene came to the airport to see me off. She said she hoped Egoitz was interested in someone else so he wouldn't be hurt when he heard the news that she'd married Fernando. Sh-she even gave me a picture of Katalin."

There was another slight pause, and Miguel wondered what was going through her mind to produce the unreadable expression on her face.

"When were all of you planning to let Irene in on your secret?" she demanded.

Miguel cursed under his breath. Revealing one truth had turned everything into a nightmare of staggering proportions. "When were you and Irene planning to let Egoitz in on *hers?*" he whispered.

Chastened, Nickie didn't have an answer for that.

"I'm just thankful Irene loved you enough to destroy herself on that witness stand for you." Before Nickie looked away, Miguel saw the glimmer of tears. He struggled to find the right words. "God knows your suffering has been infinite. But so has Marieli's and Egoitz's.

"Irene's testimony that she and Fernando were married the same night you offered to baby-sit Katalin undermined the one point in the case that could have carried any weight in the countersuit—it proved you went to our house for no other reason than to help out a friend. It also turned everything around for Marieli and Egoitz. They've been caught in this situation for fifteen years, condemned to grabbing a little happiness when and where they could. And all the time, Egoitz has felt overwhelming guilt because he had to act the devoted fiancé to Irene. Nickie—" he paused, trying to find the words. "I know this has all come as a great shock."

Nickie's mouth tightened. "You mean the same way Marieli has had to pretend to love *you?* Was she still playacting the night she screamed at me that I'd destroyed your marriage, that I'd almost killed your baby?" Her tormented cry reverberated throughout the store.

Without conscious thought, Miguel reached for her, cradling her hot face to hold her still. Scalding tears poured down her cheeks onto his fingers. "Listen to me. You don't know any of the circumstances that prompted her outburst."

"I don't want to know," she said in an agonized whisper. "The idea that either of you could think I'd neglect Katalin or do anything to harm her—"

Miguel froze in place. "What are you talking about? Where did you get the idea I blamed you for anything that happened to Katalin that night?" When she wouldn't look at him he slid his hands to her shoulders and shook her. "Answer me! Who said I was upset with you?"

"No one said anything. They didn't have to," she moaned. "It was the angry way you looked at me. The way your eyes condemned me."

He blinked in surprise, remembering that night. He and Marieli had met secretly with Egoitz, only to learn a shattering piece of information that had sent them racing back to the house much earlier than planned.

The shock of walking into his living room and discovering a flushed and guilty-looking Nickie, instead of Irene, standing next to John Forrester, would live with him forever. Irene had told him repeatedly that Nickie wasn't interested in John, in fact went out of her way to avoid him. But that wasn't how it looked from Miguel's perspective.

Forrester's predatory behavior and Nickie's obvious discomfort had stirred visions of what they must have been doing before he and Marieli interrupted them. It tore him apart. Until then he'd never seen Nickie deliberately flirt or act provocatively around another man. He'd had no idea John Forrester had finally managed to worm his way into her affections.

Never in his life had he known such jealousy, been so filled with rage. If he'd ever needed proof of his feelings for Nickie, he had it that night.

"If I didn't trust you with my life, would I have allowed you to tend the baby on those other occasions? Whatever you thought you saw in my eyes, it had nothing to do with your care of Katalin."

She shook her head. "Don't pretend with me, Miguel. I know you too well. Haven't there been enough lies for one lifetime?"

She tried to pull away from him, but his hands sank deeper into her sweater until he could feel the heat from her body. The scent of her hair and skin intoxicated him, drowning him in sensation. The more she struggled, the more he tightened his hold until she stopped fighting him.

"I know all this has come as a tremendous shock to you, Nickie, and I don't blame you for wanting to have nothing to do with me. But on the strength of our long-standing friendship, will you please listen to me?

I haven't begun to explain everything yet. And there's something of vital importance I have to ask you."

After an eternity had passed, she said in the coldest voice he'd ever heard, "I forgive you, if that's what you're worried about."

"Now who's lying?" he retorted. "I've known all along that once you learned the truth, you'd never be able to forgive me. That would be asking too much. But you have to hear me out, and I'd prefer talking to you over dinner where we can sit down and be comfortable. This is going to take some time."

"There's nothing more to say and I really don't know why you bothered to come here. Obviously Irene could have told me everything when she felt the time was right. I have other plans for the evening and I'm already late. Since my car's parked behind the store, I'll let you out first and then lock up."

"That's not what your aunt said. She indicated that you'd be going straight home after work for an early night. I told her you'd be late."

She pulled completely away from him. "You had no right to do that!"

"That's true," he admitted calmly, more determined than ever to make her listen. He followed her back to the counter where she'd stowed her purse. "I've never had a right to do any of the things I've done to you. But I swear I never meant to hurt you. And some day soon Marieli and Egoitz want to explain everything and beg your forgiveness. You need to know that the night Marieli and I treated you so cruelly, we did it for your own protection."

He heard her sharp intake of breath and watched the way she slowly shook her head, her expression one of total disbelief.

"Yes, Nickie. It's true. We *had* to push you away and make sure you stayed away until everything was resolved. But after you left the house, I realized we'd gone too far, that you needed to be told the truth before you were hurt beyond reparation. Marieli agreed the situation was out of control but pressed me to wait until after we'd met with our attorney the next day before I talked to you.

"As soon as our meeting concluded, I left for Tahoe and drove directly to your house, only to discover that my worst fears had been realized. Your parents told me you weren't home, you'd gone away. Under no circumstances would they reveal where you could be reached. That was the blackest night of my life. For a time I nearly lost my mind trying to discover your whereabouts.

"I alienated Irene by accusing her of not giving me a phone number or address where I could get in touch with you. When she swore she didn't know where you were, I didn't believe her. That's when I hired a private detective to trace you. He found you at your aunt and uncle's but when I called them, they refused to speak to me. They said that if I came near you, they'd get a restraining order."

That revelation appeared to surprise her. "They hadn't told me," she said quietly.

Miguel hid his fists in his pockets. "If it's any consolation, I haven't known a moment's peace or happiness since then, nor have Marieli and Egoitz. Nickie, now that I've caught up with you, you have to listen long enough to hear the whole explanation—if not for my sake, then for theirs.''

"None of it matters anymore, Miguel. It's over.''

"No,'' he said fiercely. "That's where you're wrong! And until you've heard everything, we'll stay here all night if necessary.''

Her mouth twisted mutinously. "You mean if I won't listen, you'll use your size and strength to get your way?''

"Is that what I do?'' he asked, his voice now expressionless.

She shrugged uncomfortably, then looked away. "Go on.''

"Originally Marieli and I had planned to stay married a year, then get a quiet, uncontested divorce. We felt that if we lived together twelve months, it might satisfy both sets of parents that we'd tried to make our marriage work. And the financial settlement would resolve an old land dispute between our two families. That's something I'll explain in a few minutes.

"But when Marieli realized she was pregnant, it threw our plans into chaos. In the first place we had to convince Egoitz that Katalin was his. We decided it would look better if we put off the divorce until after the baby was born. Egoitz was desolate because it meant more delays, more anguish.

"The night I asked Irene to baby-sit was the night Marieli and I flew to Zack's ranch to meet with Egoitz. We'd initiated divorce proceedings, and they could finally begin to make plans for their own wedding. We had great cause to celebrate.

"But when we got there, Egoitz was already waiting for us with the worst possible news. Our secret was out! Marieli's family had gotten wind of our impending divorce and they were in an uproar.

"As you know, Egoitz's parents are good friends with the Echevarrias. He overheard them talking about a conversation they'd had with Marieli's cousin, who learned of our petition for divorce through a friend who works for the Second District Court and happened to see the file.

"But what turned it into a tragedy was finding out that her family blamed the breakup of our marriage on *you,* Nickie. Egoitz found out that Marieli's family intended to ruin your life, the way they were convinced you'd ruined their daughter's marriage.

"When we heard that, I phoned my attorney, but she was out for the evening. Zack flew us back to Reno and we went over to her house to wait for her. When she arrived, we told her what we'd learned and asked her to find a way to speed up the divorce before Marieli's family could make their move against you. I told her that, above all, I didn't want you hurt or brought into this."

As he spoke, Nickie clutched the purse tighter to her chest. Miguel couldn't be sure, but he thought that at last he had her attention, that she was listening.

"She said she'd do everything possible to keep you out of it. In the meantime, she told me to stay away from you. We couldn't afford to let anyone point a finger. She warned me to avoid the slightest hint of suspicion."

He raked an unsteady hand through his hair. "Do you have any idea how I felt when we walked in the house and discovered *you* there, instead of Irene? With John Forrester, of all people, the biggest gossip in the department? So many questions ran through my mind and I couldn't ask one of them."

Nickie must have sensed his turmoil because she lifted her head, her eyes haunted.

"I knew John was intensely jealous of any attention you paid to me, Nickie, that he wanted you badly enough to make the worst kind of trouble and exploit it to his own selfish ends.

"Marieli and I have always been able to read each other's minds. It comes," he said with a wry smile, "from years of subterfuge. In a split second we knew what we had to do. While I got rid of John, Marieli laid into you, hoping to scare you off until we had word from our attorney that the divorce had gone through."

"She was very convincing," Nickie said in a pain-filled whisper. "It was horrible."

"It was meant to be horrible. You have to understand that Marieli and I would have done anything to protect your name. *Anything!* She looked at the situation as a godsend and decided to say the baby was sick to frighten you off, to make sure you stayed away until we'd obtained our divorce.

"She would never blame you for Katalin's condition. But you ran away before I could get to you. The fact that you'd left believing all those lies has made it impossible for any of us to find happiness."

"I had no idea," she admitted, subdued, her fingers torturing the straps of her handbag.

"Of course you didn't," he returned. "What normal human being could understand the kind of intrigue and deception that drove Marieli, Egoitz and me? The agreement drafted by our grandfathers years ago threatened to destroy all our lives unless we found a way around it."

Nickie took a shuddering breath. "Why did they do such an inhuman thing to you? Didn't they know you can't govern other people's lives that way?"

"*Their* marriages were arranged and seemed to work out. They assumed Marieli's and mine would, too, but ours had special strings attached. What I'm telling you now, very few people know about. It has to do with the family dispute I mentioned earlier."

He sighed heavily before continuing. "After the turn of the century, Marieli's great-grandfather, the most prosperous man in the village, lent my great-grandfather a good sum of money to go to America. In return, my great-grandfather was supposed to buy property for both of them and to safeguard it until Marieli's great-grandfather could join him.

"My great-grandfather ended up in Nevada. Apparently he did well and started a restaurant in Carson City. Later he bought up property around Lake Tahoe. But he was unscrupulous and kept all the land for himself. Marieli's great-grandfather came here, expecting a land claim, and ended up with nothing. He returned to the Pyrenees, although one of his sons stayed here.

"By then there was a full-blown family feud. The two men passed down their hatred of each other to their children, and it wasn't until her grandfather and mine were in their nineties that the idea for the marriage agreement came into play.

"It was too late to work out a settlement with their own children, but we grandchildren could be manipulated. So my father and Marieli's father had to swear an oath that through a marriage between Marieli and me, half the original land would revert to the Echevarrias and all debts would be paid to restore the family honor."

"But that's archaic!"

"Yes. Now you're beginning to get an inkling of what Marieli and I have been up against from the time we were born. You know what's been written about us—that our race has a streak of hardness, that this hardness translates into contempt for weakness and an indifference toward human suffering."

"But that's only one man's opinion. Not all Basque people have lived that way."

Miguel gave another heavy sigh. "I agree, but there's a grain of truth in what he says. We come from a long line of democratic thinkers so independent they consider themselves above earthly law. The *fueros* our ancestors drew up with their feudal lords in the Middle Ages are my case in point. Every pure-blooded Basque was to be counted as a 'noble'; as such he would allow no central government official to collect taxes and would never be conscripted for the army.

"My parents were born with that same blood flowing through their veins. Basques make their own laws—for themselves and their descendants. I find many similarities between our two families and the people Caesar's armies described as the proud fierce warriors of the Pyrenees.

"Centuries may have passed, but for some people like my parents and Marieli's, nothing has really changed. They've expected Marieli and me to behave like good Basque children, to obey without question. Egoitz's story is no different. His family owed mine for some favor rendered years before, and it was decided his marriage to Irene would satisfy the debt."

"How galling for your families that Egoitz is now married to Marieli, and Irene to Fernando. Nothing worked out the way it was supposed to," she said, almost as if to herself.

"Except that Marieli deeded over the house and property to her parents, who now possess the title. We hope that's finally put an end to a bitter conflict. But you're right about everything else. Our parents refuse to acknowledge me or Irene, which comes as no surprise. Fortunately she's too preoccupied with her pregnancy to think about it right now.

"Egoitz's father told him he's no longer welcome in their home. However he's so happy to be married to Marieli that he doesn't let it immobilize him. They've bought a house in Sparks where Egoitz works, and now that the adoption is final, Katalin is legally his.

"Life has been hectic since the trial. I've had to deal with the demands of my work, of course, and with all the legal transactions, which took months to go through. Not to mention the logistics of moving two households. I helped Egoitz find the right place for Marieli and Katalin.''

There was a prolonged silence. ''Was it hard to give her up?'' Nickie's gaze slowly met his and he saw a trace of compassion enter their velvety depths. It gave him the opening he'd been looking for.

''Yes. I won't lie about that. I loved Katalin like my own flesh and blood. She brought joy into my life when there was none. On their wedding night Marieli and Egoitz took her away. It was hell watching her go, particularly since Egoitz is naturally possessive of his daughter and hasn't once allowed me to visit her. I suppose I could insist on my legal visitation rights, but—'' he shrugged ''—my mind knows this is for the best, even if my heart still needs convincing.''

''I'm sorry, Miguel,'' she whispered. ''I loved her, too, so I can imagine how great a wrench it must be for you.''

He nodded. ''Living without Katalin has taught me a lot about myself. I've found out I'm not the loner I thought I was. I'm getting older and I don't have a child of my own. I'm jealous of what Marieli and Egoitz have.''

Her strange laugh bordered on a scoff. ''Thirty-three isn't such a great age, Miguel. Men much older than you have married and had children.''

''I'm not husband material, Nickie. No non-Basque woman would come near a man like me, not with my sordid history and the whisper of scandal that will always surround me. No Basque woman will ever want anything to do with me now that I've been labeled an adulterer. You know as well as I do that to a Basque, adultery's the most heinous of crimes. I'm an outcast on all fronts, Nickie.''

"Don't say that!" Her voice betrayed a curious tremor. "The judge ruled out adultery."

"Since when does that stop the public from drawing its own conclusions? My divorce made headlines. Even the president of the college has told me that certain parties who hold the purse strings have pressured him to relieve me of my position. At this point, my job is tentative.''

"I was afraid of that," she admitted with an unexpected rush of emotion. "But you didn't do anything wrong!''

"I've done everything wrong, Nickie," he said fiercely, "and I'll spend the rest of my life paying for it. But as to the charge of adultery, you're the only person alive who knows what went on between us.''

He paused and held her gaze.

"And that makes you the only woman I could ever ask to marry me—so I can have a child to replace Katalin.'' He was aware that her feelings for him were those of a sister, not a lover, but he also knew how much family meant to her, how much she'd loved Katalin. And he knew that she would dote on a child of her own. He prayed that the possibility of having his baby would outweigh her reservations about marrying him.

For the second time that night he watched the color drain from her face. Evidently the thought of marriage to him sickened her. *Because she thought of him as a brother.* She'd said so repeatedly. It was evidently the truth. He felt as though he'd come to the end of his life.

"What an irony, eh, Nickie? To think that after all I've put you through, I'd dare ask you to marry me. When I know you're not in love with me...." Bleakly he turned away from her and zipped up his parka. "I'll let myself out."

CHAPTER SIX

AS HE HEADED for the door, Nickie stood there in a trance. If she understood him correctly, he'd just asked her to marry him.

Long before their first trip to Europe, marriage to Miguel was something she'd wanted with every fiber of her being. But he'd been Marieli's fiancé, and never once in Nickie's relationship with him had Miguel treated her any differently than he'd treated Irene.

She remembered those moments in Zackery Quinn's pool. To her shame she'd ached for Miguel to make love to her, ached for him despite his commitment to Marieli. But his reaction had proved he wasn't attracted to her. He couldn't have been, because her behavior had been too wanton for him to resist—*if* he'd been halfway tempted.

She wasn't proud of it, but she'd done everything she could think of to arouse his passion. He'd still treated her like a sister. No man could have had more opportunities to act on his desire if he had wanted a physical relationship. For years the whole world had assumed they were lovers. What greater proof did she need that the chemistry wasn't there for him?

When her mother had first told her Miguel was divorcing Marieli, Nickie's immediate fear was that he'd fallen in love with another woman; it had practically destroyed her. Part of her had wished the charge of adultery *had* been true, that she and Miguel *had* been lovers. But nothing could have been further from the truth, which made the countersuit with its charge of adultery so ludicrous.

It was the love he felt for Katalin that had driven him to want a child of his own, that had brought him to Colorado now. And the sense of emptiness brought on by his parents' desertion, plus the displacement of having to give up his birthright....

Nickie realized he'd come to her because she was the constant in his life, the only person who knew the whole truth about him. The only woman who understood his stringent code of honor, which wouldn't allow him to enter into a marriage where there couldn't be absolute trust. The kind of trust that existed between lifelong friends.

In a way, he'd paid her the greatest compliment. They *were* friends. Furthermore, they were friends who respected each other and had always worked side by side as equals.

When Nickie thought about it, many of those elements were missing in a lot of marriages. Sometimes the only thing a new couple had to cling to was their passion, and when it was spent and the realities of everyday living descended, there was nothing of substance to hold the marriage together.

Miguel couldn't promise passion, but they had everything else. And when they decided to have a child, he would treat her with dignity and tenderness—and gratitude.

The problem was Nickie wanted more than friendship from him, important though that was. She wanted, with all the passion that was in her, to be Miguel Aldabe's lover.

She moaned as a great ache passed through her heart.

If she married him, she'd have to hide the sensuous side of her nature, because if he ever knew the truth, if he ever knew how desperately she wanted him, he'd pity her. She could handle anything but his pity.

But would she be able to keep that secret from him as perfectly as he'd kept his secret from her all these years?

Nickie knew the answer to that question before she even had to ask it. She ran out into the blizzard, terrified that she was too late to prevent him from leaving. He'd already backed his rental car out of its space in the deserted parking lot.

"Miguel—" she cried, and dashed in front of him, waving her arms. "Stop!"

His car skidded sideways to avoid her, nudging her left leg so she fell headfirst in six inches of fresh powder, which hadn't been there the last time she'd looked outside.

A car door slammed.

Miguel rarely cursed in Euskara, but when he did, Nickie and Irene had always run in the opposite direction. Right now he sounded angrier than she'd ever heard him before.

"I'm all right," she said, scrambling to her feet as he approached. "Honestly. I only slipped in the snow. You didn't hurt me."

"A few more inches and I might have killed you," he lashed out. He swept her up in his strong arms and half carried her into the store. Then he shoved the door closed with the heel of his boot and put her down gently. "Whatever possessed you to run in front of my car like that?"

Nickie couldn't think, let alone talk, while he brushed the snow from her hair and shoulders. His touch electrified her, filled her with warmth.

"You left before I could tell you yes."

His hands stilled on her upper arms and his dark eyes glittered with a strange light. "What are you talking about?"

A tremor shot through her body. *Have I misread the situation?* "If you want me to marry you, I—I will."

"Why?" he fired back too quickly.

She needed more time to come up with a plausible reason that wouldn't give away her true feelings, but he wanted an answer. Now.

Before she could form words, the telephone rang. "That might be important." She jumped at the excuse to give herself more time and would have dashed over to the counter to answer it, but Miguel didn't loosen his grip.

"The store is closed, and your aunt and uncle know I'm with you, so let it ring. Tell me why you'd be willing to commit yourself to bondage with me."

"Bondage..." She laughed a trifle nervously and avoided looking at him. "Really, Miguel, you're being melodramatic. I was thinking of it more as a... partnership. In exchange for my giving you a child, you reinstate me at the college, get me back my old job at the library and help me obtain my Ph.D. in Basque studies. If you analyze it, neither of us can have what we want without the other's help."

His hands tightened on her shoulders. "I'd do that for you automatically, Nickie."

"But I wouldn't come back to the college as anything but your wife!" she said in forceful tones, realizing she meant it, and finally met his gaze without flinching. "As far as the Basque community in Nevada is concerned, I'm an adulteress. Since that trial we're both outcasts, anyway. You said it yourself.

"At least being Mrs. Aldabe will end further speculation about our relationship, and it will keep John Forrester off my back," she added on a sudden burst of inspiration, gratified to see the way he grimaced at the mention of the man's name.

Nickie knew Miguel despised John on a personal level, but he had no legitimate professional reason to fire him.

"If I were to obtain my Ph.D. I'd want to teach on the faculty, which would make John and me colleagues and we'd *have* to get along. But that would never happen if I didn't have your name and protection."

Miguel let go of her arms abruptly and put his hands on his hips. "The second I can find him another position outside Nevada, I'll send him there so fast he won't know what hit him," he vowed with a ferocity that suggested his warrior ancestry; it made Nickie shiver.

"Perhaps you can persuade Dr. Basaldua to take him on at the University of Iowa."

"I've already put the idea in motion," Miguel confessed.

"Good. I'm relieved." But her smile slowly faded as he submitted her to a piercing glance.

"Nickie, if we were to get married and I made you pregnant, I'd want you to take good care of yourself."

Miguel had always been protective of her and Irene, and she would never try to change that quality, which she found endearing. "When I discover I'm pregnant, I'll slow down a little. Nowadays most women combine children and a career. I'll be able to do some of my thesis work at home. Will you mind tutoring me sometimes?"

A strange expression crossed his face, one she couldn't decipher. "You won't always be studying, Nickie."

She hoped not. She planned to make Miguel so happy he'd *have* to fall in love with her, and she could imagine all sorts of ways they would spend their nights....

Nickie wouldn't allow herself to dwell on the possibility that she might not be able to conceive, thus providing Miguel with an excuse to divorce her.

Afraid he was already entertaining reservations and had perhaps even changed his mind, she said, "Now would be the perfect time to get married. The Christmas holidays will give us a long enough break before the next semester starts and you get bogged down with department business."

His head reared back, and she feared that maybe her intuition was right. Maybe he was having second thoughts. She couldn't let that happen. Now that he'd presented her with the opportunity to become his wife, she wasn't about to let anything get in the way.

"I'm afraid I already am inundated. January fifteenth is the deadline my publisher has given me to finish the book. When I was forced to fire you, I didn't hire anyone else to help me because no one can decipher my notes or read my mind the way you can. So everything's sitting just as we left it. If you recall, there's a portion still to be written because I haven't completed my research."

"I thought you'd already traveled to Onate!"

"If Marieli's baby hadn't come early, I would have gone there and finished things up. But nothing turned out the way we'd planned. Anyway, for the first little while, Marieli needed me to help take care of Katalin."

"Then we'll go to the Pyrenees right away and I'll help you get your book finished," she suggested eagerly. "We can be married over there surrounded by your friends from the University of San Sebastian. We'll have a real Basque wedding.

"I know you've already lived through one with Marieli," she teased, trying to coax him into a less serious mood, "but it'll be my first as a participant." Despite her intention, her voice quavered with the strength of her emotions. "I think it's one of the loveliest and most exciting of all your Basque traditions."

Her idea seemed to startle him. "Wouldn't you prefer to be married at home with your family in attendance?"

Nickie had to think fast. Naturally her parents would want to be present at her wedding, but she'd make them understand why it was so important to get married in the Pyrenees, Miguel's ancestral home.

Except for Zack Quinn, who was Miguel's closest friend, and his parents and sister, the people who meant the most to him resided in Basque country. Besides, his marriage to Marieli was a sham, part of a deception. She felt intuitively that *this* wedding had to begin in the traditional Basque way if it was to erase the falseness of his first marriage. And as far as an outsider could, she wanted to share in the Basque heritage that was so much a part of him. They'd be surrounded by his Basque friends and family....

"If we ask my parents to host a reception for us when we return, that will make them happy." Before he could raise any more objections she said, "My passport is current. What else has to be done for us to get married overseas right away?"

"Let me worry about that," he said offhandedly, still acting subdued and strangely reticent. "What about your job here?"

Thank heavens she was related to the owner. "There are a dozen applications on file right now. The local students have all come home for vacation and are clamoring for temporary jobs. My uncle will be able to fill mine with one phone call."

He sighed heavily and continued to regard her through veiled eyes. She couldn't tell what he was thinking. "You don't know what you're getting into," he began. "You're so young...."

She panicked because she could sense he was backing off. "Women younger than I am have babies every day. If you're worried about my capability as a mother, then I don't know why you brought up the subject of marriage in—"

"Nickie." He silenced her emotional outburst. "I've seen you often enough with Katalin not to have any worries in that department." He paused, rubbing the side of his jaw absently. "My concern is that one day you'll wake up and wish you were somewhere else. With *someone* else."

Her sudden pain was so acute she didn't care what she said next. All his objections proved only that he didn't love her and never would. Obviously friendship and shared goals wasn't going to be enough for him, either. "That's not what's really bothering you, is it, Miguel? I think you're already experiencing too many doubts for this to work. So I'll just forget the subject of marriage was ever brought up and get on with my plans. It would be best if you left. I have to lock up."

"What plans?" he demanded, ignoring anything else, his dark brows furrowed menacingly.

"I've decided to focus on Arabic. Remember what my counselor said? To keep that option open? Well, I've been making a lot of inquiries, and I've enrolled in a graduate program at the University of Alexandria. I'll be leaving for Egypt after the holidays."

She heard his sharp intake of breath. "Have you already paid your fees?"

"Actually, yes."

His body stiffened. "What's going on, Nickie? If you've gone that far, why did you just agree to marry me?"

She took a shuddering breath. "Because for a few minutes you gave me hope I could realize an old dream." She paused, taking time to phrase her explanation carefully. "I've been fascinated with Euskara since Irene first took me to your house and I heard all of you speaking it. Some people say we've discovered everything there is to know about this planet, but that isn't so. The origins of your language are still a mystery, and I feel compelled to try to solve it.

"When you took me to the Caucasus, I knew I wanted to pursue a career in Basque studies, but since that time a lot has happened." Her voice broke.

"One thing I've learned from the trial is that we can't always have what we want in this life. After a lot of soul-searching, I made up my mind to accept what for me is second best. I decided to study the Coptic languages because they interest me. How was I to know you'd show up this evening or...or make a rash comment you're already regretting about marrying me and having a baby to replace Katalin?"

"It was anything but rash, Nickie," he interjected gravely. "I've given it more thought than you could possibly imagine," he added more cryptically. "I just wanted to make sure you'd considered all the ramifications before you committed yourself to anything as binding as our marriage will be. Because once we have a child, there'll be no divorce."

Her eyes had been smarting and she looked away to regain control. "Well, I guess it's your decision. I've already stated I'm willing to marry you. If that doesn't happen, I'll go to Egypt. Much as I'd prefer to go back to Reno and pick up my studies where I left off, I'm afraid I'm not strong enough to return to your department and face the enmity of the whole Basque community singlehandedly.''

A tension-filled silence pervaded the store. ''As my wife you won't have to.''

For the second time in one evening Nickie's emotions took a roller-coaster ride. The dips and climbs made her dizzy. Her eyes fastened on the man who'd just made it clear he was about to become her husband, and she wondered if her heart would always beat too fast when she was near him. Would she be in a perpetual state of nervous anticipation, fearing he'd never give her his heart?

''To save time, why don't you call your folks from here with the news? Tell them we're leaving for Madrid in the morning.''

''All right,'' came her breathless response. With trembling excitement, she moved behind the counter and picked up the receiver. Long ago her parents had guessed the truth about her feelings for Miguel Aldabe. They wouldn't be shocked or surprised that she was willing to marry him, even if the love was all on her side.

''While you do that, I'll go out and warm up the car. The sooner we get you to your aunt and uncle's to start packing, the better. You're going to need warm clothes where we're traveling. Inake says there could be snow in the mountains any day.''

How many times in the past had she prepared to go away on a trip with Miguel?

How many times had she dreamed they were travelling as husband and wife, looking forward to a private interlude in some secluded hideaway in the mountains?

"Miguel?" she called to him before he'd reached the front door. "What about your parents?"

He came to a standstill but didn't turn around. "They don't have a son."

Tears stung her eyes and her throat swelled. "Do you mind if I phone Irene?"

"And if I do?"

She almost dropped the receiver. "Then I won't."

"Eskarikasio." Thank you.

He closed the door with exquisite care and went out into the blizzard.

She stared after him. A storm more terrifying than the one outside raged in Miguel's breast, frightening her as perhaps nothing else ever had.

Had Irene done the unforgivable by not confiding in Miguel that she'd married Fernando? By forcing him to learn about it in the humiliating circumstances of the trial? Had he cut her off the same way as his parents had shut him out because she hadn't remained loyal to him?

Nickie shivered when she thought of that anger, that cold disapproval, ever being directed at her.

Without wasting another moment she phoned her parents in Incline Village but got the answering machine. Frustrated because she'd have to wait to confide in them, she replaced the receiver and decided to call them later from her aunt and uncle's house.

Miguel hadn't come back in yet, so she hurried to the rear of the store to get her parka and lock up. After putting the money in the safe and turning off all the lights except those ones left on for security reasons, she dashed to the front door and let herself out knowing her uncle would take care of the car. She locked the door for the last time and put the keys in her purse.

The storm was abating. Miguel had been brushing the snow from the back window of the car, but when he saw her he opened the passenger door and helped her inside. The interior was warm and inviting.

There'd been too many winter nights in Colorado when she'd had to battle the elements by herself. It was such a thrilling sensation to realize she no longer had to do everything for herself, by herself. Nickie had to pinch herself to believe that the man she'd loved in secret for so long was going to be there to take care of her—as she intended to take care of him.

With the exception of Zackery Quinn, no man had ever anticipated her needs the way Miguel did. For years Nickie had been the recipient of his protection, which honored her womanhood and bordered on chivalry. He'd always made her feel safe and cherished, yet never condescended to or treated her as less than an equal.

In the Middle Ages Miguel would have been known as a black knight, ferocious and terrifying to his enemies in battle, but a revered lord to those who lived beneath his protection. As for the lady who held his heart, she would have been the happiest of women.

For her and her alone would he lay aside his weapons of war and take her to his great bed, where they would lie enraptured in each others arms and—

"Nickie! Which way to your uncle's house?"

Miguel had obviously called her more than once, but she'd been too immersed in her fantasy. A hot blush swept over her body. She'd never been more grateful for the darkness.

"Turn left and follow the main road for two miles. Then turn right."

He maneuvered the car through the snow with his usual expertise, relieving Nickie of any nervousness. "That was a short phone call," he said.

"My parents weren't home. I'll try to reach them later this evening." Traffic was slow because the plows hadn't been by for a while, but nothing deterred Miguel, who forged steadily ahead. "When we arrive in Madrid tomorrow, will we stay there overnight?" she asked.

"No. We'll take a connecting flight to San Sebastian. Inake and his wife are expecting me."

"I hope they don't mind that I'm with you."

He darted her a searching glance, which took on an intimacy she'd never felt before, and it made her pulse race. "You're my wife-to-be, Nickie, and they would welcome you for that reason—even if they didn't already love you. You've been a guest many times in their home." She could tell that Miguel was smiling as he said, "Inake wouldn't be happy if people weren't coming and going from his house."

Nickie held Inake Petoteguy in great affection. Not only was he one of Miguel's best Basque friends, but he'd been her professor on the summer-abroad program several years earlier. A short stocky man full of vibrant enthusiasm, he was adored by his students.

That trip the three of them had spent in the mountains was one of Nickie's choicest memories. She'd never seen Miguel laugh so much or act so lighthearted. The two men were brilliant in their field, and for the moment she'd been content to worship while she tried to learn as much as she could from them.

"Where are we going to be married? In San Sebastian?"

A trace of a smile formed at the corners of his mouth. His mood had altered dramatically since he'd gone outside to remove the snow from the car. "Why don't you let me surprise you?"

She turned her head and eyed him warily, her heart pounding hard for no good reason. "I don't like the sound of that. Your surprises are famous for turning into nightmares." The comment produced a deep chuckle from Miguel.

"It's not funny," she said. "I remember on our last trip you told me we were going to stay all night in a charming little spot only you and Zack knew about beneath the Pic du Midi d'Ossau. It was going to be a wonderful surprise.

"We ended up spending the better part of it helping some pathetic shepherd find his stray sheep who'd wandered out on a rocky ledge during a cloudburst! They smelled horrible—and I had to leave my sleeping bag behind because one of the ewes took a liking to it and wouldn't give it up!"

His chuckle turned into full-bodied laughter, and he reached over to grasp her hand. He didn't release it. The warmth of his touch radiated up her arm until it filled her whole being.

"It's not funny." She barely managed to get the words out, almost paralyzed by the intimate contact. "P-promise me you won't let your friends do something ghastly like kidnap me and lock me in a barn with a bunch of cows all night."

"I promise that if you do find yourself locked in a barn with the animals, you can be certain I'll be locked in there with you. We'll find our way to the loft where nothing will disturb us," he murmured in a husky voice.

Her answering remark was left unsaid as he lifted her hand and pressed his mouth to her palm. The sensation electrified her, preventing her from saying anything else.

CHAPTER SEVEN

THREE DAYS LATER, after a long transatlantic flight, Nickie once again found herself in another rental car with Miguel, this time driving into the Pyrenees.

Freezing rain hit the windshield faster than the wipers could dash it away. Nickie's eyes strained to make out any road signs as they drove through the mountains sparsely populated with *caserios*, the quaint farmhouses indigenous to the Basque region.

"Nickie, we're coming into Lecumberri. See if you can spot the turnoff for Leiza."

"*Leiza?*" She glanced at him in astonishment. "Isn't that the beautiful little farming town we came across while we were hiking here a few years ago?" Miguel nodded without saying anything. "Remember that deserted stone farmhouse, isolated from the rest of the town in a high meadow? We ate lunch there in a carpet full of purple and white wildflowers."

He came to a stop and turned to her, his eyes more black than brown as he studied her animated features. "How could I forget?" he mocked dryly. "You went into ecstasy. As I recall, you wanted to buy the entire farm and stay there forever. I had to literally pick you up and carry you partway down the mountainside."

"I remember." She blushed and averted her eyes from his intent gaze. She'd behaved like a foolish spoiled child, but she couldn't help it. Inake had hiked that far with them, but after lunch, he'd had to return to San Sebastian on urgent university business.

Finally she'd found herself alone with Miguel in that idyllic setting, and the euphoria had gone straight to her head. For those few carefree hours, Miguel had been especially teasing and attentive, and she'd pretended that this was their home, that they belonged to each other. When it came time to go, she'd rebelled because her heart was breaking for a love that could never be.

And all that time he hadn't felt the slightest interest in Marieli. But no one had known he was living a lie, least of all Nickie, whom he'd always treated like a cherished younger sister.

In an effort to put the bittersweet memory out of her mind she said, "If the weather's this bad here, it'll be snowing over the Huici Pass."

"Possibly," he murmured, suddenly sounding preoccupied and distant. She didn't know what to make of his erratic mood swings. Earlier in the day he'd been as charming and entertaining as the Petoteguys, their congenial hosts, while the four of them enjoyed a delicious breakfast together on the patio of their elegant turn-of-the-century home.

In Nickie's honor, the Petoteguys had included *churros*—strips of fried dough dipped in a cup of thick hot chocolate. She found the food too sweet for her taste, but Miguel couldn't get enough. She suspected that they'd really provided the *churros* for him.

Miguel had always had a sweet tooth and inevitably stopped at Juncal's in San Sebastian for a box of their famous chocolates, which he usually ended up eating himself. As far as she knew, it was his only weakness; he drank alcohol in moderation and never smoked cigarettes. On rare occasions, he smoked a pipe, but usually only when he was thinking out a serious problem.

After arriving at the Petoteguys by taxi two nights before, Miguel had immediately closeted himself with Inake while Nickie had gone straight to bed and slept round the clock. Midafternoon of the following day, she and Lore, Inake's wife, had gone shopping for a variety of important items, including Nickie's wedding dress.

After hours of searching, she'd finally found what she wanted. Later, the four of them had spent a "tourist" evening dining on *besugo,* a native fish dish, in the old part of the city. Afterward, they'd ridden the cable car to Monte Igueldo. Nickie still trembled when she recalled how Miguel had unexpectedly moved behind her and drawn her against him. It had been while they were looking out over the spectacular panorama of San Sebastian, renowned for its shell-shaped beach.

His arms had gone around her like a cloak, enfolding her so that she felt every beat of his heart against her back. The longer they stood there with his chin resting in her hair, the more his heartbeat merged with hers. Soon she couldn't separate the two. She'd fought to catch her breath.

His touch had stirred something intensely alive inside her, but she feared the gesture had been solely for his friends' benefit.

So far he hadn't discussed the actual wedding arrangements with her or even indicated where or how soon the ceremony would take place. Whenever she thought about it, she started to feel afraid he would change his mind; it made her reluctant to ask.

But then she'd remember the way he had grasped her hand and kissed it that night in the car on the way to her aunt and uncle's in Colorado. The memory of that sensation left her hot and confused.

It was the first time he'd ever purposely done anything to physically arouse her. He'd known exactly what he was doing when he lowered his mouth and suckled her palm. Her heart had almost stopped beating. Until then, she'd had no idea a woman's hand could be that sensitive to a man's touch.

This practiced intimacy led her to believe there had been other women in his past, despite what his attorney had claimed about his chaste behavior. It brought out her jealous streak, particularly because he'd kept his private life so private she couldn't even imagine who those other women were.

She'd suspected for a long time that Ana Guevera had been in love with Miguel. Possibly they'd had a short affair, which might explain why Ana had been willing to sign that affidavit for Mr. Aranburu.

A man Miguel's age wouldn't have remained celibate all those years, a fact that pained Nickie because he'd never once tried to kiss *her* or make love to *her*.

Because he'd never been physically attracted to her, she thought.

That was what hurt so much now. When he'd touched her in the car and again last night, he wasn't acting out of passion or desire. Logic told her that. Until he made her pregnant, every kiss or caress he gave her would be for a purpose—part of a role he was playing.

And no one could play it better than Miguel. He was a master of deception with a lifetime of practice behind him.

Nickie had dated a lot in the past year and she'd been kissed on several occasions, but for her it had always been an experiment of sorts, to see if she could blot Miguel from her mind. She never could. She simply had no interest in ever making love to anyone else.

Miguel probably assumed—correctly—that she was still a virgin; he probably intended to woo her gently until he held the child he wanted in his arms. She wondered what he'd do when he discovered his naive little bride burned with desire for him and planned to please him in every possible way until he forgot he was playing a part. Until he admitted he couldn't live without her, child or no child.

"Miguel?" she murmured tentatively. "I thought you were in a hurry to get to Onate and dig into the university archives. Why are we driving to Leiza? It's out of the way."

"Because Leiza is where we're going to be married."

He spoke so calmly that at first Nickie didn't understand what he meant. When his words sank in, her fingers tightened around the edge of the bucket seat.

"But I thought you'd want to be married in Irun where you have family."

He downshifted as they approached a fork in the road. "Though Marieli and I didn't say vows in our hearts, to our immediate and extended families the marriage was a sacrament to be celebrated only once in this life. My marriage to you is my own affair."

"Maybe you're being too hasty. To a Basque, a wedding without family is no wedding at all. I don't want to be the cause of further alienation."

"What's the matter, Nickie? Is all this becoming too real for you?" He accelerated as he took the next bend. Only his coordination and swift reflexes prevented them from careering off the shoulder.

"No," she said with an ache in her heart at his obvious pain. She stared out at the narrow road winding up the mountain. "I just want you to find a little happiness."

"You and the children we have together will be the only family I need. I will be happy."

She bent her head. Now he was talking about *children*, not just one child. "What if something goes wrong...and I can't have a baby?" She'd been frightened of that possibility ever since he'd broached the subject.

His gaze left the road briefly to rest on her. "Is there some reason to think you have a problem? Something you haven't told me?"

She shook her head. "No."

"Then there won't be."

"But—"

"Tomorrow we're going to be married, Nickie. And in a little while we're meeting with the priest who will perform the ceremony. He wants to talk with us and there are some documents to sign."

With pounding heart she asked, "Does Leiza have some special significance for you?" As far as she was concerned, she'd already spoken her vows in her heart—the day they'd discovered that deserted farmhouse high up in the meadow.

"*Bai.*"

His simple "yes" told her that was all she would get out of him for now. She was left to ponder the admission in silence.

They climbed steadily, the rain turning to sleet. After they'd crested the pass, they dropped down into the tiny village of Leiza. It was a scene straight out of some ancient Basque legend.

Instead of an alpine meadow alive with wildflowers such as they'd seen the summer they'd come here, they were met by the very different sight of the Pyrenees in winter. A little snow lay in patches at the higher elevations, while the stone barns and outcroppings stood in rugged, primitive beauty below. It reminded Nickie that these mountain people were the oldest inhabitants of Europe, and their traditions reached back for centuries.

Nickie felt a quiver of pure excitement. She prayed that by this time next year she and Miguel would have a son or daughter. A child who would be heir to his birthright, another little Aldabe to complete his life.

Miguel deserved a child he could love and teach his own values to, a little boy or girl who would grow up to perpetuate his native language and culture, which were in danger of being lost.

She was so deep in thought she didn't realize they'd turned onto a side street and parked near a small medieval-looking church. The heavy Romanesque structure, with its distinctive ochre exterior, had been converted to a charming inn. Miguel anticipated her question before she could ask it. "We'll be staying here tonight."

He didn't mention where they'd be sleeping tomorrow night—their wedding night.

"How soon do we meet with the priest?" She quickly changed the subject, afraid he would sense how excited she felt.

"Not until four. We have plenty of time to freshen up and eat a leisurely lunch. They serve a delicious *ttoro* here, filled with wrasse, conger eel and bream. I think you'll enjoy it."

It was bouillabaisse, Basque style, and more than a tasty soup. Nickie recalled that it was a full meal which included a fish dish cooked in white wine, a specialty Miguel had always been partial to.

She wondered how many times in the past he'd been to Leiza to be able to recommend the inn's fare. The thought crossed her mind that he'd probably brought a woman here to enjoy a discreet weekend interlude. Maybe it was a woman he'd met on his trip with Zack, or a colleague from the University of San Sebastian.

Another, more painful thought intruded. Once they were married, how did she know Miguel would remain faithful to her? Before the trial, she would have said he was incapable of a dishonorable act.

Tortured by the pictures that filled her mind, she quickly lost her appetite and jumped out of the car before he could help her, putting up the hood of her parka as protection against the drizzle.

"Miguel, after we take in our bags and get registered, do you mind eating alone? That breakfast was filling and I need to finish up some last-minute shopping. I promise to be back in plenty of time for our appointment."

His expression didn't alter, but when he walked around the front of the car his eyes narrowed with disturbing intensity on her flushed features. He reached inside his parka and pulled out his wallet.

When she realized his intention she said, "I have money, and the few things I need won't cost very much."

There was a prolonged silence. "After tomorrow we share everything, Nickie."

Did he think she didn't know that? Didn't he realize she was living for it? Her greatest fear was that her love might not be enough to hold him, that in time he'd seek familiar comfort elsewhere. Even worse was the likelihood that if he did, she might never know.

The possibility was insupportable to Nickie, but what could she do about it? "I'll see you later, then." Avoiding his level gaze, she turned and walked away.

NICKIE'S SUDDEN withdrawal affected him deep in his gut. He'd choke on food right now. The thought of how she'd react when they met with the priest made him break out in a cold sweat. The way she was behaving, he wouldn't be surprised if she was building up her courage to come back to the inn and tell him she couldn't go through with the marriage.

His enchanting Nickie. Born with far too much compassion and a warm generous heart that bled for another person's pain. It had gotten her into real trouble this time. How valiantly she'd stated her reasons for marrying him.

He didn't buy one of them.

He knew for a fact that the only reason she'd agreed to his outrageous proposal was that he'd made damn sure she felt sorry for him. It was because he'd been ostracized by his family and because he'd lost little Katalin that she was willing to give him a child of his own. He'd counted on her love for the baby to be the deciding factor. She hadn't disappointed him.

But four days had passed since she'd agreed to marry him, and he could sense that all her noble ideals were crumbling under the weight of stark reality. If he had a shred of decency left, he'd call off the wedding.

His eyes closed tightly while he fought the battle raging inside him, uncaring of the sleet or the occasional passerby. Irene would have seen through his ploy in an instant, which was why no one but Zack knew his plans when he left Reno. He hadn't wanted Irene talking to Nickie or influencing her in any way until after the wedding.

Since the trial, his relationship with his sister had undergone a drastic change. In some ways they were closer than ever and they needed each other more, because their parents were still unforgiving and not speaking to either of them.

Yet oddly enough they were farther apart where Nickie was concerned. Irene made it clear she didn't want anything else to hurt Nickie, and by tacit agreement they didn't discuss her. If Irene knew what he was about to do, she'd try to put a stop to it, and justifiably so.

But to let Nickie go now meant never seeing her again. It was all or nothing. How could he let go of something that had grown to be a part of him?

He knew the answer. He'd always known the answer, and though he might go to hell for it, he would reach out for the bride of his heart and love her for however long she allowed him to. He hoped to get her pregnant right away. Knowing Nickie, once they had a child, she would find it difficult, if not downright impossible, to leave him.

"*Arratzalde-on,* Mikel," the proprietor greeted Miguel warmly a few minutes later. "I've been expecting you." He rushed over to the door to help him with the bags. "Where is your fiancée, Miss Brinton?"

"She's out doing some last-minute shopping. Are our rooms available now?"

"For you, of course. I've put you in the one you've always used, and as per your instructions the private dining hall in the old nave is being made ready for your wedding party tomorrow."

"Thanks, Polli. As you know, we won't be a large crowd. Sixteen people in all."

"Yes. We will be able to seat you at one table. You asked for the best wine. I'm expecting a shipment before the day is out. Oh—" he glanced in his planner "—the tower rooms are being held for the Petoteguys and your godparents, the Alderdis, for tomorrow night. Is that correct, or do you wish me to reserve more?"

"No. The other guests will leave after the dinner. They have families to get back to, and it's too close to Christmas for them to stay over."

"I understand."

Miguel took the key from him. "If you would be kind enough to take our bags upstairs, I have some business to attend to. My fiancée will probably return before I do. Please show her to her room and tell her I'll be back no later than quarter to four."

"Very good." Then Polli made a gesture and said in a low tone. "I have to tell you my wife is relieved you are finally getting married and says she can't wait to meet your fiancée. You don't know what a wife is like, but you're going to find out." His brows met. "She's seen you come to Leiza again and again over the past few years without your American woman. Her curiosity has grown greater and greater."

Miguel zipped up the front of his parka. "There have been reasons why I couldn't marry her before."

"Ah, but now the waiting is over." His dark eyes twinkled. "She will give you fine Basque children?"

Miguel's heart broke rhythm for a moment. "She's the light of my life."

"I thought it must be like that. You are a very fortunate man."

"You don't know how fortunate." Miguel's voice shook, then he smiled at Polli and strode swiftly toward the entrance.

Once outside he looked both ways to see if Nickie was coming before he climbed into the car. She would have walked to the center of town to make her purchases, even if they'd been just an excuse to get away from him.

He took a back street until he came to the road that led up the mountainside past scattered *caserios*. By the time he reached his destination, the road had become little more than a mud track, but it was still negotiable.

Collecting his three briefcases—filled to the brim with his notes and manuscript—from the back seat, he got out of the car and walked the short distance to the stone farmhouse. *His* farmhouse. He'd purchased it after bringing Nickie here the first time.

He found the key he needed and let himself in, breathing deeply of the scent of pine. The heat had been turned on, and the house was warm and welcoming.

The neighbors to the west rented his land and farmed it. In return, they acted as caretakers. They'd outdone themselves when they'd learned he and his bride would be honeymooning there.

Outside, they'd stacked an enormous pile of wood. Inside, a perfect pine tree stood in the far corner. In a few days, he and Nickie would decorate it and enjoy their first Christmas together in their own home as husband and wife.

Glancing around, he noted all the special touches and put down his cases to explore. A ceramic bowl filled with a variety of flowers purchased from a local greenhouse sat in the middle of the gleaming wood dining table. New handwoven curtains in a simple blue-and-brown pattern were drawn back from the window, revealing the valley below.

On the kitchen counter stood a magnum of fine French champagne and two etched-crystal glasses with slender stems. Touched by his neighbors' thoughtfulness, he wandered through the house, which had taken two years to remodel.

In the beginning, he'd had two walls knocked out to enlarge the fireplace and living room area, part of which he used for a study. He'd also combined the kitchen and dining areas, and he knew Nickie's taste down to the color of the stain she'd have wanted on the wood beams.

The original farmhouse was small and contained only one bedroom and bathroom. He'd had a loft and half-bath built over the far end of the living room; it was reached by a circular staircase. Three, even four twin beds could be set up there to accommodate children.

He opened the door to the master bedroom opposite the dining area. A larger window had been put in so they could lie in bed and have an unobstructed view of the mountains.

Every time they'd hiked in these mountains, Nickie had begged him to sit down for a while in an alpine meadow and enjoy the view with her. But he'd always refused because the temptation to take her in his arms had been too great. Particularly the afternoon he'd spent with her here on this very spot after Inake had left them. That was when Miguel had come close to making his first serious mistake. He'd realized it would be dangerous ever to be alone with her again.

But that was in the past. This was now, and she could watch the sunshine turn to thunder while he watched her. His heart leapt in his chest when he imagined kissing her mouth and making love to her beautiful body—the body that had tantalized him for too many long, unfulfilled years.

He'd almost forgotten why he'd come to the house. Slowly, he slipped one hand into his pocket and took out a gift, which he slid under one of the pillows beneath the bedspread.

His other wedding present, wrapped in brown packing paper, lay propped against the massive carved armoire, a seventeenth-century piece he'd bought at an auction in Pamplona.

Everything was in readiness. All that was required was his bride.

He wandered over to the window and looked down at the village below, hardly aware of time passing. Nickie was there somewhere. He had to clamp down hard on his fear that when he returned to the inn she'd tell him, in her slightly breathless voice, that she'd changed her mind and wanted to go back to Colorado Springs.

"Do you have any idea where he went?" Nickie asked the proprietor in Euskara, panic-stricken because it was quarter after four and Miguel still hadn't come. They were already fifteen minutes late for their appointment with the priest.

"He said he had something important to do and would be back soon. Why don't you go in by the fire and wait?"

Nickie nodded and took his advice, all the while berating herself for not having accepted Miguel's invitation to lunch. He expected to marry a mature woman, not a silly, lovesick child who was jealous of every woman in his past.

Five minutes after she'd left, Nickie had realized her mistake and run back to the inn to tell him she was sorry, that she wanted to have lunch with him. But he'd already gone. She was so shocked, so frightened by his unexpected departure, she'd dashed up to her room and burst into tears the minute the door was closed.

The next three hours had felt more like six. A shampoo and bath took up only a portion of the time. She was ready long before they needed to leave and lay on the bed in her black slip, unable to read or concentrate because she kept listening for the phone or a tap on the door.

When it drew close to the hour, she dressed in an elegant two-piece black wool suit lined in silk, which she'd bought while out shopping with Inake's wife. The jacket fastened with two large jet buttons, and Lore had persuaded her to buy a matching necklace and earrings.

Miguel very rarely made personal remarks, but he'd once mentioned that black set off her fair skin and hair. Ever since, she'd hugged that little observation to herself, taking it as a compliment of sorts. She wanted to look beautiful for him; she wanted him to be proud of her.

With her suit she wore black leather heels that added a couple of inches to her five-foot-five height and made her feel more confident when she stood next to him.

"Nickie?"

At the sound of Miguel's deep voice she whirled around, searching his face for some sign that he'd forgiven her. But every thought fled as his gaze made a sweeping appraisal of her hair and figure, igniting that core of heat inside her. His eyes seemed to smolder like dark flames, until she realized they were reflecting the firelight.

"I've been waiting hours for you," she said. "You must have left just before I came back."

"You've been waiting hours?" His question held undercurrents that left her uneasy.

"Yes. I..." She hesitated, afraid to tell him the truth, that her jealousy had gotten out of control. He'd probably call off the wedding. "I changed my mind."

No trick of light could produce the sudden loss of color that left his face lifeless. Maybe he was ill. "Miguel, are you all right?"

"Why did you wait this long to tell me?" He sounded so unlike the man she'd always known she felt suddenly afraid.

"How could I when I didn't know where to find you? The car was gone and the proprietor had no idea where you were."

His mouth contracted to a thin line. "I warned you that you were too young and inexperienced to know what you were getting into. I was a fool for not taking my own advice."

Nickie started to tremble. "Please, Miguel. Can we just forget it and go see the priest now? I'm sure he's wondering what's keeping us."

A stillness came over him. "Now what are you saying?"

"Maybe I should ask you the same question," she retorted in a hurt voice. "Maybe you're late because you've had time to think and you've changed *your* mind."

"What in the hell are you talking about?"

She couldn't look at him. "I realize it wasn't very nice of me to turn you down for lunch, but I didn't think I was hungry until I started walking. That's when I hurried back to—"

"Nickie." He broke in, raking long fingers through his hair as if he'd reached the limit of his endurance. "Somehow I get the feeling we're talking at cross-purposes. You think I was upset because we didn't have lunch together? Is that what you're saying?"

"I wasn't sure. When it got to be quarter after four, I worried that maybe I'd offended you in some way and that you were having second thoughts about . . . about everything." Her voice trailed off and she glanced at her watch. "It's already twenty to five. Do you think the priest will still see us today?"

He blinked. "You're dressed like that to see the *priest?*"

She frowned. "If you think it's inappropriate," she said hesitantly, "I'll change, but that'll make us later than ever."

Like someone walking underwater, he slowly moved toward her and lifted the necklace to his gaze. His fingers grazed her neck and the hollow of her throat where the heat mingled with her perfume and she could feel her own erratic pulse.

"I've never known a woman with better taste," he murmured in a husky voice. "Surely after all these years you realize that. When I saw you just now I assumed..." Once again flames seemed to flare in the depths of his eyes. "Well, it doesn't matter what I assumed.

"Give me five more minutes and I'll be ready. My errands took longer than I'd planned. But the priest knows we were driving from San Sebastian today, and he won't be unduly concerned unless we don't show up at all."

He let go of the necklace and the beads seemed to burn her skin. After he left the room, Nickie sank into the nearest chair. The weakness she felt had little to do with the fact that she hadn't eaten since early morning. It had much more to do with the way he'd spoken to her just now, the way he'd looked at her.

His eyes had seemed to engulf her, and the sensuality of his touch... For a moment, he'd acted like a man in love.

Acted, a little voice reminded her, bringing a shudder.

The day he looked at her like that, the day he touched her like that and *meant* it, that was the day

she was living for. Never again would she do anything
to jeopardize their relationship.

Full of new resolve, she got up from the chair and
walked into the reception area, smiling at several
tourists checking in at the desk while she waited for her
husband-to-be.

CHAPTER EIGHT

NICKIE DIDN'T WANT to say good-night when Miguel accompanied her to the door of her hotel room. After their meeting with the priest, who was totally understanding about their delay and discussed the arrangements for the ceremony in detail, Miguel had taken her to a local bistro. They'd eaten the most delicious hake in a green sauce and homemade pastries, Basque style, that melted in your mouth.

Afterward they'd walked back to their hotel, talking companionably the way they used to do, soaking up the atmosphere. But when Nickie's heel caught in a crack, he'd put his arm protectively around her shoulders. He left it there, so that their hips and thighs kept brushing. Nickie thought she couldn't bear it if he didn't satisfy the ache growing inside her—if he didn't kiss her, something she'd been waiting too long to experience.

Out of all the couples in the world preparing to be married the next day, she imagined she was the only bride who wouldn't know the taste of her husband's mouth until their wedding night.

If Miguel had any idea of the intensity of her desire for him, how eager she was to lie in his powerful arms and make love, he would be shocked. She actually felt so feverish with anticipation she wondered if she might be running a slight temperature.

Afraid he could tell, which was a humiliating thought, she didn't linger outside the door. She immediately busied herself searching in her bag for the room key. When she'd inserted it into the lock and opened the door partway, she thanked him for the lovely dinner and bade him a hasty good-night.

"Are you aware this is the last time we'll be together until we meet at the altar tomorrow?" he asked in a solemn voice before she could shut the door.

She clung to the handle for support. "I didn't know. In that case, wait just a minute. I have something for you."

Leaving him standing there, she dashed into the room for the specially wrapped present she'd bought him in San Sebastian. "Here," she said, returning to the doorway. When she handed it to him, she couldn't be positive but she thought he seemed pleased.

"Since it's bad luck to see my bride on the day of our wedding until the appointed hour, shall I open it now?"

"Yes," she said, wishing her heart wouldn't beat so fast.

He removed the paper and opened the box. Inside the tissue nestled a new black *txapela*. Miguel lifted the waterproof beret in his hand to admire it.

"It's for you to wear tomorrow. I—I hope you like it. I found it in an old elegant men's shop on a little side street near the Basilica Santa Maria."

She watched the way his fingers caressed the material and could imagine how they would feel against her skin. Without warning, he looked up and caught her staring at him. She flushed.

"This is a priceless gift because it comes from you, Nickie. I'll wear it with great pride." His voice sounded thick, as if he was caught in the grip of some deep-felt emotion. She *had* pleased him!

"The Mass will be celebrated at noon, so sleep in as long as you like. Breakfast will be brought to your room whenever you let the desk know. I'll send Karmele to help you dress."

"Karmele Alderdi?" she said excitedly. Karmele was one of the nicest women Nickie knew. She and Irene had loved visiting her and her husband whenever they traveled to Irun.

"Yes." His eyes gleamed with satisfaction. "Miraculously, my godparents have not forsaken me and are looking forward to seeing you again. José will drive you to the church and give you away. Karmele will accompany me."

"That's wonderful. I'm so happy for you, Miguel."

"I have to admit I'm pleased, but I realize you'd rather have your own parents with you."

"It's all right. They understand we had to combine our wedding with business, and they couldn't possibly have gotten passports in time. I'm going to phone them tonight so they'll feel a part of everything, and I'll call them again tomorrow evening. Lore promised me she and Inake would take videos of everything inside the church and at our wedding party. My whole family will love those."

She would have shut the door, but he stood in the way, his eyes veiled so she couldn't read his thoughts.

"Nickie, make sure your bags are packed before you leave for the church. After the ceremony, we'll come back here for our wedding lunch, then be off."

"Will we be driving to Onate?" she asked in her brightest voice, but inside she wilted. All this time she'd thought they'd be staying at the inn for at least one more night before he got back to his research.

"A good Basque bride doesn't ask questions like that of her bridegroom." There was humor in his tone but Nickie didn't smile.

After a brief pause she said, "I promise to be a good wife to you, Miguel."

"Just be Nickie," he returned back with an urgency that caught her off guard. *"Gabon."*

"Gabon," she whispered, and shut the door, sick at heart because he couldn't even bring himself to kiss her good-night.

Just be Nickie.

She fell back against the door. Was that his way of warning her not to assume too much? That even though he was marrying her for a child, he'd made no pretense that this was a love match and didn't want her building expectations he could never meet?

Aware she was dwelling too much on that aspect of their marriage, Nickie hurried over to the bed and put through a call to her parents from the phone on her bedside table. They'd been anxiously waiting for her call and sounded relieved to know that Karmele was going to be there for Nickie in their stead. She finally ended the conversation, promising to call again the next day, after the wedding.

She longed to phone Irene, as well, but for some reason Miguel didn't want her calling his sister. She wouldn't dream of going behind his back when she'd already given her word. After their wedding tomorrow, she'd ask him the reason and hoped Irene would forgive them both.

THE CHURCH in Leiza appealed to Miguel by virtue of its small size and simplicity, which he found more beautiful than the gaudy ornate shrines of the large cities.

Though it was almost noon, it felt like early evening. The weather was cold and overcast, creating a somber atmosphere throughout the interior of the church. Without the sun's penetration, the reds and blues of the stained-glass windows resembled dark jewels.

The priest, garbed in rich vestments, entered from a side door while Inake and Lore stood close by taking pictures.

One by one, Miguel watched his other good friends enter the nave and take their places in the pews near the front. How he wished that Zack could have been among them. But much as Zack had always hoped to be present at Miguel's wedding, Alex was pregnant with their second child and having such a difficult time with morning sickness, she couldn't travel. She and Sean needed him at home.

As Miguel stood there, listening to the full rich sounds of the organ music, he pondered Zack's parting advice. "You don't have time to wait where Nickie's concerned. Act now or you might lose her forever."

The terrifying thought that even now she could back out made his heart thud painfully. Every time the rear doors opened, he anticipated seeing her standing at the entrance on the arm of his godfather, José. Yet every time one of the invited guests appeared in the doorway, instead, fear gnawed at his insides. What if she didn't come? If that happened, if she left him, he'd never be able to endure the rest of his life.

A hand patted his arm. "She'll be here, Mikel." Years of familiarity made Karmele able to read his mind. "She loves you."

"Like a brother," Miguel said in a haunted whisper.

Her hand tightened on the sleeve of his suit. "If you believe that, then you're not the brilliant man everyone gives you credit for being."

"You don't know what I know, Karmele."

"And you don't know what I know, my foolish son. Ah. Here they are now."

For Miguel it was as if the sun had suddenly burst forth, filling the church with golden light, and all of it radiating from the honey blond woman standing at the back.

Gowned in heavy white silk, wearing a lace mantilla that draped her head and shoulders and fell beyond her slender waist, she reminded Miguel of an exquisite medieval maiden. The lace over her forehead framed her dark eyes and emphasized her warm coloring. Her classic beauty drew admiring gasps from everyone assembled.

He forgot to breathe as he watched her grasp his godfather's arm and walk toward the altar. The music swelled and seemed to him as unbearably, sweetly beautiful as his bride. To his satisfaction he noted that in her left hand she carried the bouquet of wildflowers flown in from North Africa, which he'd had specially made for her.

Afraid to touch her for fear he'd reveal the depth of his emotions, he didn't clasp her hand when she came to stand next to him.

Instead of the glorious smile that normally broke out on her face when she was happy or excited, she presented a picture of reserved solemnity and only afforded him a brief enigmatic glance before facing the priest. *Like Joan of Arc being led to the stake?*

Halfway through the Mass, the actual wedding ceremony began. Nickie's responses sounded low and weighted, and to Miguel's ears, like those of someone going to her own execution.

Gripped by a curious combination of pain and elation, he listened for the words he'd been anticipating for more years than he could remember, the words that said they were now husband and wife. Finally, minutes from now, he would kiss her for the first time.

The priest nodded to him. "The time has come for the exchange of tokens."

Miguel turned to Karmele, whose outstretched palm held the ring he'd purchased during that trip to the Caucasus. One afternoon when they'd taken a break to wander through the ancient streets and shops of Tbilisi, Nickie had been particularly attracted to a white-and-gold cloisonné ring and matching locket on display in a small jewelry store. They were reputed to have come from Russia during the time of the last czarina and were much too expensive for Nickie's budget.

Before leaving for the States, Miguel had gone back to the shop, and without Nickie's knowledge, bought both pieces of jewelry, hoping that one day he'd have the right to give them to her.

Eager to see if she remembered, he faced his new bride and guided the ring onto her finger. Her eyes were averted, but before he'd even let go of her hand, her composure slipped and he heard a slight gasp. She lifted her head, her expression one of shocked wonder.

Her eyes mirrored her confusion; they seemed to be asking him a question. The priest cleared his throat to get her attention, and Miguel watched her cheeks redden before she turned to José, handing him the bouquet. Then Miguel felt her small cold hand reach for his and slide a heavy gold band, inset with onyx all the way around, onto his finger.

He'd never worn a ring before, but the weight felt perfectly natural. He studied her bent head as she concentrated on slipping it over his knuckle and nestling it into place.

The black stone, rather than a ruby or a sapphire or even a diamond, would have been his own choice, and he marveled that Nickie knew his taste so well. The ring would always serve as a reminder of this moment; he would never remove it.

When she would have taken her hand away, he clasped it to his chest, wanting to warm her. His compulsive gesture sent a nervous tremor through her body, and her reaction plunged a dagger in his heart.

On a swift intake of breath, he lowered his head and found her lips, which dutifully met the pressure of his. But they remained closed and there was no answering warmth, no fire. She could as easily have been kissing Zack or Inake.

Nickie drew back before he was ready to let her go. Miguel sensed she would have preferred to avoid any physical contact, but she allowed her hand to remain in his—for the sake of appearance, he realized.

The priest conducted the rest of the Mass, which passed in a blur to Miguel. He was too aware of the woman who was now his reluctant wife to be aware of anything else. Before he knew it, the Mass had come to an end, and the music of the recessional filled the small church.

Nickie reached for her bouquet and, without so much as a glance at Miguel, walked down the aisle with him past his friends, who could no more take their eyes off her than he could.

Inake was already in position and taking pictures as they emerged from the church. Within seconds it seemed that everyone had clamored around, besieging them with hearty congratulations. Miguel was loath to let go of her hand but had no choice.

His male friends surrounded Nickie and moved in to kiss her on either cheek, then clapped him on the shoulder, murmuring their envy of the wedding night to come. One of the more outspoken of the group quoted loudly from the old ballad, *"Uso Txuria Errazu."* "The dove is beautiful in the air, but she is more beautiful on the table." His remark brought laughter from everyone.

Nickie's grasp of Euskara was nothing short of amazing, but she was still learning. So he wasn't surprised when her gaze darted to his and she asked for an explanation.

He pulled the beret she had given him out from his suit jacket and set it on his head at an angle. Not

wanting to disappoint his friends, he answered in
Euskara, projecting his voice. "Tonight I intend to
help you understand."

His remark delighted them and they burst into more
raucous laughter and teasing, unaware of his inner
turmoil—and hers. When he saw that Nickie's cheeks
had turned crimson, he felt a stab of remorse. He
gripped her elbow and helped her quickly down the
steps to the car, where José and Karmele were waiting.

As he leaned over to arrange the hem of her dress so
it wouldn't get caught in the door, he whispered, "In
case you're still worrying, no one's going to kidnap
you and lock you in a barn." In a more fervent tone he
added, "I'm your husband now and I'll never let you
out of my life."

Nickie hoped not, since she had no intention of letting him out of hers. Ever. In fact, her resolve to hide
her feelings from him was fast proving impossible to
carry out.

Nickie had never noticed any man but Miguel, and
today was no different. Dressed in a midnight blue suit
and white shirt, he was at his most darkly handsome.
He wore the beret at a rakish angle that emphasized
the lean masculinity of his face.

She wanted to stare and go on staring, but she had
to practice restraint in front of the Alderdis. The older
couple provided a distraction and engaged both her
and Miguel in lighthearted conversation on the short
drive back to the inn.

Karmele knew that Nickie was heart-wrenchingly in
love with her godson. When they'd been alone earlier, while Karmele was helping Nickie into her wed-

ding dress, the older woman had been shockingly blunt, almost primitive, in her ferocious affection for Miguel.

"If you do not love my Mikel down to the very marrow of your bones—" she pounded her own breast, her dark eyes flashing "—then you are not worthy to become his bride and I will not allow this marriage to take place."

With those words, Miguel's godmother had won Nickie's complete devotion. She'd raised her eyes and looked steadily into Karmele's. "If I hadn't loved him to the very marrow of my bones for the whole of my life, do you honestly believe I would commit myself to this marriage? A marriage he proposed only because he wants a child, now that he's lost Katalin?"

"Ah," the older woman exclaimed. She then muttered something in Euskara Nickie couldn't quite catch, then a knowing smile replaced her fierce expression. Without another word she leaned forward and cupped Nickie's hot cheeks in her hands, kissing her forehead in a benediction that promised to keep the admission a secret.

For a painful moment Nickie wished it could have been Begona Aldabe giving Nickie a mother's heartfelt approval, but it seemed that was not meant to be.

"Now I can part with this," Karmele had said mysteriously and pulled from her handbag something that looked like a small flat leather wallet.

Nickie's excitement had grown when she realized it was a picture holder. With less than steady hands she opened it and immediately dissolved in tears when she saw two old photographs inside the frames. They were both of Miguel; one must have been taken at his christening, the other when he was about five.

Nickie had thrown her arms around Karmele and sobbed quietly on her shoulder while she gave way to her joy and the long-suppressed emotions of a lifetime of loving in secret.

Now, when Nickie, Miguel and his godparents arrived at the inn, she discovered all their guests were already there and waiting at the entrance, ready to take more pictures.

The photographers' flashes dazzled her as she alighted from the car. Miguel came around to help straighten the skirt of her wedding gown, which brushed the stone tiles, then offered her his arm. She felt wounded anew at the impersonal gesture and the impassive expression that accompanied it.

But she made an effort to look joyful as they made their way inside, past the smiling proprietor and his wife. Several guests staying at the hotel nodded their congratulations, as well.

Miguel led her to another part of the inn, which had once been the nave of the church. Now it was converted into a dining hall with a long refectory table, big enough to seat the entire wedding party. Candlelight reflected from dozens of white tapers set in ornate crystal candelabras, creating a sense of warmth in a room that otherwise might be austere with its rounded stone arches and small stained-glass windows set high in the walls.

An intricate white lace cloth that looked like a priceless heirloom and had probably been furnished by Karmele for the occasion graced the table. It added an elegant old-world charm. That, plus the many other personal touches—such as the miniature bridal bouquets set above each plate of Sevres china—moved Nickie deeply.

Miguel had done everything in his power to create beauty for her wedding day. He'd even included Karmele and José to help ease her nervousness. Everything was perfect—and that was exactly why her pain had grown so acute.

If only Miguel loved her the way she desperately wanted, *needed,* to be loved!

But she had to face the fact that he wasn't in love with her. And though every new manifestation of his kindness and generosity made her suffer a little more, she absolutely refused to spoil this day, not when he'd gone to such great lengths to make it memorable for her.

Putting a carefree smile on her face, she accompanied Miguel to the center section of the table. He helped her arrange her dress as she sat down and placed her bouquet in front of her plate. José sat to one side of Nickie and Miguel on the other, with Karmele on his right.

When all the guests had found their places and the wine had been poured by the staff, José got to his feet and proposed a toast. "To my godson, Miguel, who has always made me proud. To Nickie, the ray of sunshine who has blessed his life. May they give me many little great-godchildren to read stories to in front of the fire on long winter nights."

Afraid to observe Miguel's reaction, Nickie smiled while the others laughed and cheered and emptied their glasses. Unused to alcohol, she took a tentative sip. The fruity red wine burned its way down her throat and started to warm her.

Nickie had awakened without an appetite and she knew she'd never be able to finish a whole glass or eat more than a few mouthfuls of appetizers now being served—delicious-looking garlic-and-shrimp pastries followed by pasta with wild mushrooms.

One thing she'd observed about Basques—they loved good food and loved any reason to eat it. She marveled at everyone's capacity, particularly her new husband's. His appetite didn't seem at all affected by the fact that it was his wedding day. It was with great relish that he ate the many courses of vegetables and clams and trout crepes that were brought to the table.

A new round of drinks accompanied every toast, which was given by one of the male guests between courses. After the succulent entrée—lamb roasted in a wood-burning oven—Inake got to his feet and smiled at *her* before speaking.

"A few years ago Nickie took a couple of my classes at the university and I got to know her as the beautiful brilliant young American scholar of Euskara Mikel had recommended so highly. She won everyone's heart.

"When she accompanied Mikel and me into the mountains, I could see how well suited they were. To be frank, I was elated when Mikel called and told me Nickie had accepted his marriage proposal." He sounded more serious than she'd ever heard him, and Nickie had a strong suspicion he'd guessed her guilty secret even back then.

"Lore and I wholeheartedly approve of this match and are delighted to discover that Mikel has the good common sense to marry the right woman. To you!" He nodded to both of them. "May your love never stop growing." He ended by draining his glass, and the others joined him.

Just as she heard Miguel murmur something in Euskara that she didn't understand, a dance troupe of fifteen people in red-and-white costumes made a lively entrance.

For the next half hour Nickie sat fascinated by their skill and passed up the dessert of lemon sorbet in champagne to watch. José kept her fully occupied explaining the intricacies of the various steps. Fascinated though she was, Nickie began to worry that her husband had forgotten her.

Until she felt a hand brush her thigh and grasp hers beneath the table. "Are you enjoying the entertainment?" Miguel murmured close to her ear.

"Very much." She knew her voice sounded shaky; it was the way she felt whenever he was near.

"This is Inake's contribution. They're the best in all Eskualherria. As soon as they finish this last number, we'll be leaving."

Suddenly, Nickie's heart tripped over itself. Tonight was their wedding night. In a little while she'd be alone with Miguel.

Her gaze returned constantly to the wedding ring that adorned her finger. Not for the first time did she wonder where he'd found a ring so similar to the one she'd admired in a shop window in Tbilisi several years earlier. There had been an exquisite locket, too. A matched set.

It was amazing that he'd remembered it at all. . . .

She was so caught up in her thoughts she didn't realize the dance had ended or that the guests were clapping their enthusiastic approval.

"Let's go, Nickie." Miguel rose from the table and helped her to her feet.

Karmele reached for Nickie's wedding bouquet. "I'll keep this for you until you return from your honeymoon."

If only there was going to be one. A *real* one.

"Thank you for everything," Nickie whispered to Miguel's godmother, hugging her again. "Thank you, everyone," she cried, but Miguel wouldn't let her linger, which elicited more teasing comments from the male guests.

He caught her around the waist and ushered her toward the door. The dance troupe had gathered there and joined hands to form a human bridge. She and Miguel had to lower their heads to run beneath it.

Everyone followed them outside, where their rental car stood parked on the quiet street. It occurred to Nickie that the day after tomorrow was Christmas Eve and the figure of Olentzero in his blue checkered scarf and black cape would be carried down streets like this all over the Basque country, while his helpers tossed candy to the children. Nickie wondered where she and Miguel would be by then. Would she be watching the scene from a hotel balcony wrapped in his arms or—

"One more picture for posterity! Kiss your bride!" Inake's voice sounded above the rest, breaking into her thoughts. Miguel must have heard him, but he ignored Inake and reached out to open the passenger door for her. Nickie had to blink away sudden tears. *He can't even bring himself to kiss me for the camera.*

The way he'd been ever since their arrival in Leiza, those two magical moments in Colorado Springs and San Sebastian when he'd acted as if they were lovers might never have been.

CHAPTER NINE

MIGUEL DROVE them to the outskirts of the village, then pulled to a stop at the side of the road. Nickie didn't understand why—unless he was being considerate of her while she removed the mantilla and laid it across the back seat so it wouldn't get wrinkled.

The car clock said 5:05, which meant they had at least an hour of near daylight to make it to Onate, Miguel's destination. It was an old picturesque university town and the center of Basque learning.

He removed his beret, tossing it on the mantilla. Then, his wrists resting on the steering wheel, he turned his head in her direction. "If you could go anywhere in the world to spend this night, where would it be, Nickie?"

Startled by his question, she didn't answer immediately. "There are so many places I like," she finally said, "it would be impossible to decide."

"I'm talking about a place you love more than any other place you've ever been." The seriousness of his tone surprised her.

"More than any other?" She smiled, trying to understand him and lighten his mood. "I'm afraid that particular place isn't available, so I'm perfectly happy to stay in Onate."

"Humor me."

Something in his voice alerted her that he wasn't willing to let it alone.

"W-where would *you* like to go?"

He eyed her through shuttered lids. "Tonight's your night. I'm in the mood to indulge your every desire."

"You've already done that." Her voice trembled; she had no idea how to react to this whimsical side of Miguel. It was so unlike him.

"Everything about today has been perfect. The purple and white wildflowers in my bouquet..." She spoke haltingly. "They took me back to that summer when we hiked up here. And this ring..." Her throat closed up and she had to swallow several times. "You remembered. It's so beautiful. Very much like the one that..."

"It *is* the one, Nickie."

Her heart leapt in her breast. "When did you buy it?" she whispered, trying to remember the details of that trip, trying to comprehend what it all meant.

"The day before we left Tbilisi, while you were doing some research. I've always intended to give it to you. I've been waiting for the right occasion."

She ran her thumb over its satiny surface. "Thank you. I'll treasure it forever." Unable to help herself, she leaned across the seat and kissed his smoothly shaven cheek, which smelled faintly of the musk cologne he favored.

She thought he stiffened at her touch and she quickly sat back again, furious with herself for being too open, too forward. Miguel had always been a very private man. From now on she would remember and allow him the space he needed.

"You still haven't answered my question."

"I'm afraid it would be beyond even your power to grant."

"Why don't we find out?" he suggested forcefully.

"Miguel, this is silly. You know I don't care where we go as long as—" She stopped before she gave herself away completely.

"As long as what?" he prodded.

"As long as we can get back to Onate in time to finish your research and put your manuscript together by the deadline," she improvised.

"We'll worry about that later. I'm talking about tonight. Our wedding night. There'll never be another one like it in the whole of our lives. That's why I want it to be memorable for you. Name the place and we'll go there. Shall we fly to Greece, Naples, Paris, Tahiti, Sydney, Rio? Or perhaps you'd rather go home to Tahoe." He sounded deadly serious.

"No!" she cried out impulsively. "The truth is, there's no other place in the world I'd rather be than right here."

"You mean in the Pyrenees?"

"I mean in Leiza. Don't you remember? The moment I saw this spot I fell in love with everything about it, especially—" She caught herself before she revealed too much of her secret fantasy.

A strange silence filled the car before he spoke. "So you'd rather stay here. Is that what you're saying?"

"If you would," she answered in a tremulous voice. "The inn is lovely. I'd just as soon go back there."

"Leiza appeals to me, too, but if I had my wish, we'd spend the night in a meadow."

She blinked in astonishment. "You mean camp out? Like we did a few years ago?"

"Not exactly like that," he said wryly. "For one thing, Inake won't be with us."

Nickie knew Miguel loved the mountains, but to camp out on his wedding night? In the middle of winter? "How could we do that? We don't even have any gear. In this weather we'd need warm sleeping bags and a tent and—"

"I've already made provisions," he assured her, "in case we decide it's what we want to do."

Was that the reason he was late for their appointment with the priest yesterday? Because he'd been purchasing *camping equipment?*

Her hands twisted convulsively in her lap. If he'd been in love with her, Nickie couldn't imagine anything more thrilling than to sleep with her husband on that mountain she'd made her own. Heat coursed through her just at the thought of their bodies entwined inside a sleeping bag, no matter what the weather. But she had the terrible feeling they'd sleep in separate bags, as they'd done before.

Maybe that was what he wanted.

She stared blindly ahead. The more she thought about it, the more she was convinced he'd never had any intention of spending a romantic night in a conventional setting like the inn. Certainly the last thing he wanted was to fly off to some exotic vacation paradise for lovers. His question had been a mere formality. A romantic gesture without substance.

Her pain intensified as she realized that despite his need for a child to replace Katalin, he obviously found the idea of making love to her repugnant. He hadn't touched her since their brief kiss at the altar. Even then, his lips had brushed hers with an almost clinical detachment. And after that, any physical contact had been initiated by her.

"Where exactly do you have in mind to camp?" she asked in a dull voice.

"If that farmhouse is still deserted, we could shelter inside."

At the mention of the farmhouse, a low moan escaped Nickie's throat. "I'm sure that someone lives there by now. It was too charming to be left vacant."

"There's only one way to find out. Would that make you happy, Nickie?"

She bit her lip. Mingled with his question was an underlying eagerness he couldn't disguise. If she said no, he'd be disappointed, though he'd never admit it. After the beautiful wedding day he'd given her, the least she could do was go along with him on this.

"Of course," she answered with feigned enthusiasm. "But first I think I'd better phone home. Mom and Dad will be expecting a call."

"We'll have plenty of time to do that after we've checked things out," he muttered quietly, then started the car.

To anyone else his response would probably have sounded normal, but Nickie had been around him too many years not to recognize tension when she heard it.

She'd promised her parents that she'd let them know as soon as she'd become Miguel's wife. They were waiting anxiously for word—they'd have a bottle of champagne cooling, they'd told her, and would celebrate her marriage as soon as she'd called—no matter what time it was. Nickie was eager to get the phone call over with, since she knew they'd be celebrating something that didn't really exist. A marriage for love....

The silence grew more profound as Miguel drove onto a dirt road that didn't seem much wider than their car. Soon they'd left the town behind and joined another road bordering the rain-soaked field and leading to the meadows above. She could picture the same terrain at the height of summer when the wild-flowers were in bloom. She could even smell them— until she realized it was the flowery scent from her bridal bouquet, which still lingered on her hands and the bodice of her wedding dress.

Out of the corner of her eye she could see Miguel's striking profile, and it brought back another memory. He was standing in the sun, the flower-scented breeze lifting the hair from his tanned forehead. She remembered staring at the thin white T-shirt plastered to his hard chest and the way his well-worn leather shorts molded his lean powerful thighs.

Miguel had always blazed their trails through the mountains, while she followed. He never knew the hours of enjoyment she'd derived just watching his tireless gait and the play of hard muscles in his calves.

He'd always been incredibly beautiful to her. Beautiful in a dark, adult, masculine way. When she was younger, she hadn't understood why she was so fascinated by him, by the shadow of his beard, or the unexpected white smile that sent tiny lines radiating from the corners of his eyes.

Not until her teens did she recognize his inherent sensuality for what it was. It made her want to touch him, lie against him with her arms wrapped around his hard body.

A surge of desire for her husband left her feeling breathless and weak. She quickly turned her head to look out the passenger window.

They kept climbing higher, until she could no longer detect any signs of civilization. And then she saw it— the sturdy, isolated stone farmhouse silhouetted against the darkening sky.

Miguel pulled to a stop.

On closer inspection, the house looked different from what she remembered. Exterior shutters, which hadn't been there before, flanked the windows. A winter woodpile had been stacked to the eaves and the caved-in front entry had been replaced with a solid-looking door of wood and iron.

"There's smoke coming from the chimney, Miguel. Obviously people are living here now. They've made the place absolutely beautiful." She took a deep breath. "We can't stay." She tried to mask her deep disappointment at finding the place occupied, though there was no evidence of a car or farm animals. Before she could guess his intentions, Miguel got out of the car, came around to her side and opened the door. Freezing-cold air rushed in, reminding her they were at a much higher elevation.

"What are you doing?" she asked, mystified by his behavior until she saw the intractable look on his face. "No, Miguel!" She panicked and shrank from him, but he caught her up in his arms.

"You've cooked something up with your friends, haven't you? Inake and the others kept grinning at me while we ate. Please—this isn't funny anymore!" She pushed against his broad shoulders, but her puny strength only made him laugh. And when Miguel laughed, he was pretty well irresistible. It wasn't fair!

He carried her high above the wet ground, taking care not to let her wedding dress drag in the mud. She struggled against him to no avail. He was so much bigger and stronger.

"All that talk about camping out was just a ruse to get me up here, wasn't it?" She talked faster and faster, terrified he and the others had planned this crazy scheme as part of the wedding festivities. She'd heard plenty of stories and wouldn't put it past him.

Still he refused to say a word, and she fought him in earnest, more disturbed by their physical proximity than anything else. They had reached the front door of the farmhouse.

Out of desperation she cupped the side of his face with her free hand and made him look at her. But that was a mistake, because it brought their mouths too close together and made her ache for his kiss.

"Don't do this, Miguel," she beseeched him. "I don't want to be separated from you. You promised you wouldn't let anything like this happen."

His eyes wandered slowly over her upturned face and his smile faded, to be replaced by a look she'd never seen before. A thrill of excitement passed through her as he lowered his head and kissed her eyes, nose, mouth. She felt a quickening deep inside, but it was all over much too soon.

"What I promised," he murmured in a husky voice, "was that if you were locked in a barn all night I'd be locked in there with you. Reach into the pocket of my shirt, Nickie. You'll find a key."

Swallowing hard, she slid her hand from his cheek to the inside of the suit jacket. Though he'd played and teased with her in the past, there hadn't been this accompanying intimacy.

His firm, muscled chest was warm to the touch. While she searched for the key, she felt his heartbeat with the ends of her fingers. He sucked in a breath; his chest heaved against her palm. She hurried to get a hold of the key, afraid he'd grown tired of holding her.

"Put it in the lock and turn it to the right," he said, his voice muffled by her hair.

She would have done it, but some intuition told her she'd been wrong in her assessment of the situation. *Totally and completely wrong.*

Adrenaline poured into her bloodstream. "Miguel?" His name came out on a shaky whisper. "Whose home is this?"

She waited, but there was no answer. Suddenly the truth shot through her like a lightning bolt.

The farmhouse belonged to him. *Her* farmhouse. It was all starting to make sense.

No wonder Leiza had special significance for him. Now she could understand why the innkeeper and the priest were so friendly. From the start, both men had been on a first-name basis with Miguel. She should have picked up on that, but she'd been too bemused by the recent events that had transformed her life to think clearly. He must have come here many times before. It explained how he knew where to find the best places to eat, why he knew exactly which road to take up the mountain.

Her shocked gaze flew to his. "H-how long have you owned this place?" she asked when she could find the words.

"I'll answer all your questions as soon as I've carried my bride over the threshold. Open the door, Mrs. Aldabe."

Mrs. Aldabe. Nicole Brinton Aldabe. Nickie Aldabe. Her new name. She felt giddy, and with clumsy fingers finally managed to get the key in the lock and turn the handle. Miguel did the rest, then swept her inside.

So many emotions flooded through Nickie she trembled. Miguel must have assumed she'd shivered from the cold; he carried her past the kitchen to the living room area, where a fire blazed in the stone hearth.

"You need warming up."

She thought he finally meant to kiss her, really kiss her, and lifted her head from his shoulder to meet him halfway. Instead, he lowered her to the floor and stood behind her while he rubbed her arms and shoulders.

It reminded her of other times, when he used to warm her the same way around a bonfire on the Circle Q after a long horseback ride. That meant there was nothing personal in his action, nothing intimate. It was something he'd do for a friend, a sister. Her pain and disappointment grew until she couldn't bear his touch a second longer.

"How did you come by this?" she asked, pulling away to inspect the double-seated, high-backed chair placed next to the hearth. She ran her fingers experimentally over the carved solar symbol.

"It's been in the Alderdis family for several generations," he said quietly. "Since they couldn't have children, they decided to give it to us for a wedding gift. Karmele told me José hopes that when we have children, he'll be able to play grandfather and entertain them with stories from that chair."

Nickie clung to the dark wood and faced Miguel, a dozen questions clamoring to be answered. He kept talking about children, but his behavior with her was no different than it had been for years, except for a few calculated aberrations that made no sense to her. He didn't act like a husband, like a lover.... "Why did you buy this farmhouse?" she asked abruptly.

He threw another log on the fire and wiped his hands. Without looking at her he said, "Why don't we talk after you've phoned your parents? I know how much you've missed them." He sounded unbearably remote as he glanced at his watch.

"It's already nine in the morning over there and they're probably getting anxious to hear from you. The phone is in the bedroom off the kitchen. While you do that, I'll bring in the things from the car and lock up."

In her preoccupation and pain, Nickie had forgotten about her parents and felt ashamed that Miguel had to remind her. "All right," she murmured. As she headed in the direction of the phone, she only superficially took in the unadorned Christmas tree and charming surroundings. Her wedding gown floated over the dark brown, highly polished wood floor.

It was like walking through her own dream. A dream she'd had again and again, ever since discovering Leiza and the farmhouse several years earlier.

Miguel had remembered everything about their conversation that day, about the changes she'd make if the place were hers. After shutting the bedroom door she noted that he'd even remembered to enlarge the bedroom window to enhance the view of the mountains.

Which meant he'd had the farmhouse remodeled long before he'd asked her to marry him. Had he coldly calculated his marriage proposal as far back as his divorce in September? Or even before that?

Why? Why had he done it? Why had he given her her heart's desire?

Was it somehow to make up for the love he didn't feel?

Nickie knew Miguel better than almost anyone did. He had a methodical, fastidious nature that never left anything to chance. He was also honorable to a fault. In return for her promise to bear him a child, he had done everything in his power to make her happy—to compensate for the one thing he couldn't give her.

She flung herself across the bed, burying her face in her hands to smother her sobs. She'd thought she could go through with it, but now she knew she couldn't. Without love, their marriage was a travesty.

"Damn your honor, Miguel. Damn you for not loving me," she cried into a pillow she'd grabbed from beneath the spread to stifle the sound.

When she heard the front door close, she realized he'd come back into the house. Fearing he might walk in on her, she quickly sat up and reached for the phone.

The call went straight through, and the second she heard her mother's voice, Nickie's tears started again. "Mom?"

"*Honey!* We've been waiting. Just a minute. Let me call your dad to the phone."

"Not yet," Nickie said urgently, turning away from the door so the sound wouldn't carry. "I need to talk to you for a minute."

"Has something gone wrong, Nickie?"

"No. Everything's been perfect. We were married at noon and then had a lovely lunch at the inn with all of Miguel's friends and his godparents."

"Then why do you sound like it's the end of the world?"

Nickie took a shuddering breath. "Because it is. Oh, Mom, I've made the worst mistake of my life and now I don't know what to do."

"Are you alone?"

"Not exactly. Miguel is in the other room and I don't know how long I can talk." She spoke in a hushed tone.

"Just tell me what's bothering you, honey."

"H-he doesn't love me, Mom."

"Of course he does. Miguel Aldabe is the one man I know who would never get himself into a situation unless it was exactly what he wanted."

"But he's never *said* he loves me! He treats me like he's *always* treated me and Irene. He's n-never even k-kissed me properly."

"Did you tell him your true feelings when he asked you to marry him?"

"No. I didn't dare say anything b-because I was afraid he'd change his mind and I'd lose him if he knew how I really felt."

"Oh, Nickie. Don't you realize there has to be total honesty between two people for a marriage to work?"

"I know that now," she half sobbed into the receiver, afraid to tell her mother the terms under which they'd both agreed to get married.

"It's possible Miguel thinks you still love him like a brother, that you aren't sure of your own feelings. After all, he's older than you are, and he more or less looked after you and Irene for years. Maybe he doesn't realize how much your feelings have changed. Maybe *he's* afraid."

"Mom—I could never marry a man I didn't love body and soul."

"I know, honey. That's the way you've felt about him since you were a teenager. But he doesn't know that, because you've kept all those feelings hidden. It seems to me you've both been less than honest with each other. I don't see that you have any choice but to tell him the truth."

"If I do, I'll lose him."

After a slight pause her mother said, "If you're so certain he doesn't love you the way a man should love his wife, then he was never yours to lose in the first place."

Nickie gripped the receiver more tightly and pondered her mother's advice. "You're right, Mom. Thank you. Give Daddy my love and tell him I'll call again soon. Right now I've got to go in and face Miguel."

"I'll pray for you, honey."

After Nickie had hung up the receiver, she buried her face in her hands again and wept quietly, trying to find the courage to go to Miguel and tell him the truth. When she did, it would be all over.

She had no idea how long she sat there, but it was dark in the room by the time her tears were spent and she was ready to talk.

Before leaving the room, she turned on the lamp so she could see to straighten the bed. As she started to put the pillow back in place, her eye caught a little flash of something metallic half-hidden in the fold of the top sheet. Curious, she leaned over to see what it was and plucked a locket on a chain from its resting place.

She gasped when she realized it was the exquisite white-and-gold cloisonné locket that matched the wedding ring.

Memories of that day in Tbilisi came rushing back. She could still hear Miguel telling her he'd buy the locket for her and she could repay him later. But she'd told him she couldn't accept his generous offer. Not only on principle, but because the locket was the kind of gift a woman wanted to receive from the man who loved her.

The man who loved her.

Nickie started to shake. The locket slipped to the floor and she bent over to retrieve it. After several frantic attempts to release the catch, she finally got it open.

Inside were pictures of two faces.

His and hers.

CHAPTER TEN

SHE HEARD A KNOCK on the door. "Nickie? Are you all right?"

In a mad scramble, she slid the locket under the pillow and finished making the bed so he wouldn't know what she'd discovered.

"Yes."

"Somehow I don't believe you," she heard him mutter. He stormed into the bedroom, his shirt unbuttoned at the neck, his tie and jacket gone.

She didn't recognize the man who stood before her, scrutinizing her swollen eyes and tear-washed cheeks.

His hair was disheveled and the character lines in his face had deepened, providing her with a glimpse of the years of suffering he'd endured yet managed to cover up. The man she'd once accused of being a stoic was nowhere in evidence. Raw emotion leapt from his burning dark eyes and dominated every part of his tense body.

A liberated Nickie walked toward him, no longer afraid of the truth.

"Miguel—would you mind undoing my dress for me? I was on the phone longer than I'd planned and I'd like to change into something more comfortable." She presented her back to him and waited with pounding heart to feel his hands on her body.

A full minute went by before he complied. One by one he unfastened the long row of buttons, taking care not to let his fingers brush her skin. "You were crying. Don't try to deny it."

"Brides do that on their wedding day."

"I heard you sobbing to your mother, Nickie," he told her in a pain-filled whisper.

"Joy affects people differently." Without waiting for a response she said, "Would you mind bringing in my suitcase? I'd like to put on my nightgown."

"You don't have to pretend anymore."

She struggled to keep a straight face. With her back still toward him she said, "All right, then I won't." In the next breath she slid the top half of her dress down to her waist and then stepped out of it completely. She walked over to the massive hand-carved armoire and hung the gown inside. Then she removed her shoes and put them away, too.

She didn't have to look to know that Miguel's eyes followed every movement of her semiclad body. She could feel their heat as they took in the modest underwear and lace-trimmed slip, which ended at the knee.

Many times he'd seen her in bathing suits that showed considerably more flesh, but he hadn't been her husband then.

"Nickie." His voice was hoarse. "Stop trying to be brave for me. You have nothing to fear. I promise I won't do anything you don't want me to."

At his words she turned around and flashed him a beguiling smile. "You want a baby and so do I." Her voice caught as she looked up at him. "I hope it happens tonight."

His face seemed to lose color. "Why? So you can fulfill your duty and be done with it?"

His question revealed the depth of his agony. He *was* afraid, just as her mother had said. He had no idea she loved him.

Nickie ran a hand through her hair to smooth it. "Is that how you feel about making love, Miguel? That it's a duty?"

His hands were balled into fists against his hard thighs.

"Nickie—"

"Is there something in your Basque heritage that forbids a man to enjoy sex with his wife except to bring a child into the world?" she persisted. "Because if there is—" she paused, amazed to see the effect of her words on him "—then I'm afraid you married the wrong woman."

"What in the hell are you talking about?"

"Simply that I've been looking forward to making love with you for a long, long time. Probably much longer than your conservative Basque nature would consider decent. And for some reason, which I haven't quite figured out, you seem reluctant. Unless this is your idea of a joke."

Miguel looked like a man who couldn't take much more—exactly what she wanted to see.

"You know very well how worried I've been about your friends doing something awful to me on our wedding night. But now I can see that, instead of letting them lock me in a barn all by myself, you've decided to mete out a much worse punishment by not touching me at all on the first night of our marriage."

"You actually think I'd do that to you?" His voice had lowered several registers.

"I don't know. I've never been married before, let alone to a Basque. Was Inake this cruel to Lore on their wedding night? Tell me this is the usual treatment and I'll stop worrying that you don't love me."

His chest heaved. "You think I don't love you?"

"I'm beginning to wonder," she said in a voice she could no longer hold steady. "Inake wanted a picture of us kissing in front of the church, but you chose not to hear him. The only other possible reason I can think of for the fact that you still haven't made love to me is that you're a virgin. Your attorney implied as much."

"Lord!"

"I'm one. It's nothing to be ashamed of." She went on talking, pretending she hadn't heard his exclamation. "I've never let another man touch me, Miguel, because I couldn't. You're the only one I've ever wanted. Most of the time I hated you for it, because my feelings got in the way of any other romantic relationships.

"It was galling to hear John Forrester testify that he knew exactly how I felt about you. But the only part of his testimony I can fault is his use of the word 'infatuation.' It doesn't begin to describe the depth of my love for you."

With that admission, his face underwent a drastic change. The lines seemed to disappear, and a light shone from his eyes.

"The priest advised us not to hold anything back," she said quietly, "so we'd start our marriage off right. The thing is—" she moved a little closer to him because he seemed rooted to the spot, incapable of doing anything more than drawing breath, and even that seemed difficult "—if I'm wrong," she went on, "and you've been with other other women in the past, I forgive you. Which doesn't mean to say I like the idea. In fact, I despise it—and any woman who's ever meant anything to you. That's why I didn't want to eat lunch with you yesterday, because everything in the town seemed too familiar to you. I was filled with jealousy because I assumed you'd been to Leiza with other women. Lovers." She surprised a look of disbelief in his expression.

She lowered her eyes. "I'm an awful person, really. You don't know what my deepest thoughts are, what I'm really capable of. If you did, you'd run as fast as you could in the other direction."

A tiny muscle pulled at the corner of his taut mouth. It was all she needed to see before taking hold of his hands and clasping them together so she could kiss them.

"To be perfectly honest," she murmured against his fingertips, staring at the rapid rise and fall of his chest, "I harbored an irrational hatred of Marieli the first time I heard she was already promised to you. And when I grew up and realized why I felt the way I did, I spent my life plotting ways to get rid of her, none of them legal or moral, while Irene spent her life falling in and out of love with the latest rock star."

Miguel shook his head incredulously.

"Since I knew you were already spoken for, I had no other choice but to stay close to you any way I could think of. Marieli's attorney was right. I'm guilty of almost every count listed in that complaint and so many more he didn't even know about."

Her voice trembled with tears. "I don't think God will ever forgive me for the sinful feelings I've had about you all these years."

"Nickie—"

"Do you know that when I heard the charges, I wished we *had* been lovers?" she cried, baring her soul. "I wished you'd taken me to bed all those nights we were alone in Georgia. I want to be the woman in your life.

"And the night we camped here—inside the farmhouse, when it was still deserted? I waited till you were asleep, then I crept over and lay down on the floor next to you and watched you for most of the night, pretending you were my husband. I prayed you'd wake up and reach out for me. You never did.

"But the worst was the night of Zack's party. I almost broke down and begged you to take me back to your room and make love to me. I didn't care if it was your engagement party. I was so in love with you that the only reason I didn't suggest it was that you gave no sign you wanted the same thing.

"Oh, yes," she assured him when his eyes probed hers, "I had it all planned. I was going to offer myself to you for the night. I was prepared to grovel, but that awful kiss you gave me on the forehead defeated me."

"*Maitea*." The husky murmur seemed to come from his soul. My beloved. The word she thought she'd never hear from his lips.

"Then you fired me from the library, and that was when my nightmare really began. Up to that time, I'd been able to really be with you as much as you would allow it. When you let me go, I was desolate. I even went to a doctor because I knew I hadn't been behaving rationally for years. I couldn't even sleep anymore.

"He told me you'd become an obsession with me and advised me to drop out of school and move away to make a new life for myself. I hated his advice and stopped going to see him.

"Instead, I kept up with my classes on the off chance that we'd run into each other once in a while. The rest of the time I simply existed. I continued torturing myself until the night you and Marieli came home and found me with John."

She swallowed. "The look of loathing on your face accomplished what nothing else could have done. My only thought was to leave Tahoe and never come back. Then, eight months later, I got that summons and I was terrified, because I was going to have to pay for the sin of loving you."

"That summons was my only link to you. Thank God you had to obey it," he said on a groan. He picked her up and carried her the short distance to the bed, then followed her down.

His mouth covered hers and the thrill of being consumed by such fierce hunger created an overwhelming sensation Nickie had never known before. It swept through her body like spontaneous combustion, stirring her soul and arousing depths of passion that no longer lay dormant. This was her husband—loving her, filling her, driving her to pour out the love she needed to give him.

"MIGUEL!"

Her scream almost made his heart fail. He dropped the towel he'd been using to wipe off his shaving cream and dashed into the bedroom. At six in the morning it was still too dark to distinguish more than an outline of her body beneath the covers.

"I'm here, darling. What's wrong?"

"Oh, Miguel! When I woke up just now I reached for you, but you were gone!" Nickie said in an agonized whisper. Suddenly she burst into heart-wrenching sobs. "It scared me so much!"

He closed his eyes to cover his emotions, still trying to absorb the wonder of Nickie's love, the depth of her capacity to give and go on giving until he felt immortal.

Removing his robe, he lifted the covers and slid in next to her, enfolding her with his body, marveling anew at the exquisite feel of her, the perfume of her skin. He buried his face in her hair and rocked her in his arms to quiet her. "After what we've shared, do you honestly think I could stay away from you?"

She nestled closer and kissed him with deep urgency. "It's *because* of what we shared that I was so terrified to wake up alone. If you ever left me..."

"I love you, Nickie. You're my whole life. Surely after last night you can be in no doubt of it."

"I can't hear you say it enough. Do you think it's possible to love a person too much? I don't even want to let you out of the bed."

"Not even to shave? I'm afraid I've already given you a rash. That's the only reason I left you at all."

Her fingers caressed his smooth jaw, then she followed with her mouth, inflaming his passion. "I love

your beard. I love everything about you—everything...."

"Nickie." He said her name with longing, still
finding it difficult to believe she was his wife, that she
was safely locked in his arms, that they had the rest of
their lives to love each other like this. "I can never get
enough of you," he murmured against her throat,
seized by a primitive desire that drove him to love her
with almost savage intensity.

A long time later, when the gray light of another
overcast day filled the room, he felt her stir and lifted
his head so he could look at her. "*Ongi etorria,* Mrs.
Aldabe. Welcome to my life."

She answered him with a tremulous smile. They lay
facing each other, her cheeks and forehead still flushed
from their lovemaking. He never tired of studying her
features and those velvety brown eyes, which gazed at
him adoringly. "Miguel, do you know how wonderful it is to be able to look and take my fill of you—
without fear of giving myself away?"

"I have some idea," he said in a wry tone. "Remember, I'm older than you are, and I've been
watching you and hiding my attraction to you for
years now."

A sadness crept into her expression. "You were so
strong. I don't know another person with your kind of
self-control."

He slid a hand into her hair, enjoying its silky tex-
ture. "That's because you were the prize I was waiting for, working for. I didn't dare make mistakes,
because it meant I'd risk losing you."

Nickie blinked and raised herself up on one elbow.
"You planned to marry me all along?"

She was too far away. He pulled her close and kissed her beguiling mouth. "You've always been there in the background of my life, Nickie. But when the three of us—Irene, you and I—went to Europe the first time, I began to realize my feelings for you had undergone a change.

"I didn't like it when every man, young or old, made passes at you. Inake was crazy about you, and I experienced my first taste of jealousy when he flirted and you flirted back. He made you laugh. I didn't like it at all. That was when I made up my mind—one day you and I would be together."

"Is that why we left his house so abruptly that time?"

"So you remember. He was engaged to Lore, and I didn't want him forgetting it."

"But I was only seventeen."

"You were a woman at seventeen, Nickie, and utterly desirable. All my Basque friends had their eye on you. From that time on, I pursued you ruthlessly while I waited for you to grow up."

"You never pursued me. It was the other way around," she confessed in a quiet voice. "Much as I loved learning Euskara, I'm afraid you were the greater part of the attraction."

How blind they'd both been! "I guess I never told you I broke all the rules by suggesting you come to work in the Basque library for me. I passed over a dozen applicants who had far more qualifications in Basque studies and library skills than you, gifted as you are. John Forrester knew something was going on, which was why he never quit trying to cause trouble."

Miguel could tell his admission had shocked her. She pushed herself to sitting position. "You shouldn't have done that!"

"I couldn't help myself. I was a desperate man." He pulled her back down to him. "I wanted you near me as much as possible and I couldn't think of a better way. What made it so perfect was that it gave me a legitimate excuse to ask for your help with my book. Not only did we work incredibly well together, but it meant your evenings would be tied up so you couldn't date other men."

He kissed her astonished mouth, then nudged her onto her back. "I kept watching for some sign that would tell me you were in love with me, too, but that sign never came, Nickie."

"Never came?" She gazed up at him in sheer disbelief. "My love for you was transparent enough for the whole world to see. Why do you think I moved in with Irene when we started college? It wasn't just because we were friends. Rooming with her was the next best thing to rooming with you, which I knew was out of the question."

He followed the outline of her lips with his finger. "Who do you think told Irene about the rental house in the first place? A rental house that wasn't available until I made overnight arrangements, I might add. I was the one who suggested the two of you room together so you'd be closer to the campus. To me."

Her eyes widened.

"You never knew about the blazing row Irene and I had with our parents when we found out they wanted Irene to live at home and commute to the college. That meant you and she would be split up and I wouldn't see you anymore as I had in the past. I couldn't let that happen, couldn't let you get away from me.

"Little did I realize then that Irene had an agenda of her own and wanted to get away from home. She wanted to move in with you just as badly as *I* wanted her to. Between the two of us, we finally managed to win our parents around, with the proviso that Amaia join you to keep an eye on Irene when I couldn't."

"I almost didn't move in with Irene when I found out Amaia was going to room with us," Nickie admitted. "She was Marieli's cousin, and I didn't see how I could handle that."

"But you did."

Nickie nodded. "Because I knew there was no choice, not if I wanted to see you as often as possible. I knew you'd be dropping by to check on Irene, and I wanted to be there, no matter what. I loved you too much, Miguel." A tremor passed through her body. "This last year has been a nightmare. It hurts me that you and your parents are estranged from us." Hot tears trickled from her eyes. "They've always been so good to me. And I know how important family is to a Basque. To you." Her voice shook and she struggled to regain control. "Miguel, I want them to forgive us."

"They will when we present them with a grand-child. Irene's baby will soften them up. By the time ours comes along, they'll be ready to ask us home for dinner. They'll be part of our lives again."

"I hope so," she muttered fervently. "Oh. Just a minute. I'll be right back."

"Not so fast!" He trapped her with his arms. "Where do you think you're going in such a hurry?"

"I have another present for you, and our conversation reminded me of it. It's in my overnight bag. I would have given it to you last night but..."

"Last night you and I had other things to do." He kissed her lovingly. "We still do."

"This will only take a second, but you have to promise not to look."

She delighted him beyond comprehension. "How can I enjoy my present if I can't look at it?"

A rosy blush crept into her cheeks. "I meant don't look at *me*. I don't have a robe or anything."

He broke into laughter. He couldn't help it. "That's good. Let's keep it that way."

"Miguel!"

"I've been looking at you all night. How could you possibly be embarrassed now?"

"I don't know. I just am. Please. *Plazer baduzu?*"

He couldn't resist stealing another kiss. "Since you asked me so nicely in Euskara, I'll close my eyes. But only this time, and I'm counting. You have exactly thirty seconds to come back to me, or I'll come and find you. One. Two..."

He felt the mattress give and heard the sound of her feet padding quickly across the wooden floor. He continued to count out loud so she could hear him. "Twenty-nine. Thirty!"

He opened his eyes as she hurried back into the bedroom, wearing a filmy peignoir of white silk and lace.

"These are for you." She sat down on the bed next to him and handed him two small packages wrapped in newspaper. "I had them made on my last trip to the Pyrenees. I'd intended them as a wedding present for you and Marieli, but when it came time, I couldn't give them away. They held too much significance for me and I wanted them to be *ours*."

Intrigued, Miguel felt their light weight and un-wrapped the first one, lifting the intricately carved wooden figure to eye level. It bore an uncanny like-ness to his father. With an unsteady hand he opened the other package, and soon another carved figure bearing an unmistakable resemblance to his mother joined it.

"Years ago Irene explained about the small carved statues on the mantel over your parents' fireplace. She said it was the Basque way of showing respect for grandparents. I thought it was a lovely tradition.

"One day when Irene and I were visiting with the Alderdis, I told Karmele what I intended to give you for a wedding present. She put me in touch with a lo-cal wood-carver whose work is well-known through-out the Pyrenees. He asked for photos of your parents and said he'd try to make the figures look like them. He's good, don't you think?"

As she bent her head to inspect them, Miguel crushed her to him, so touched by her gift he couldn't speak. Perhaps this, more than anything else, re-vealed how totally she'd loved him all the time he'd been in hell, unaware.

Now he understood Karmele's cryptic comment at the church, when she'd told him that if he believed Nickie loved him like a brother, he was a fool.

Nickie raised her head and stared at him. "I've never seen you cry before."

He took a shuddering breath. "I've never been as moved before. You're the light I've sought in the darkness, Nickie. I swear I'll love you till the day I die.''

Needing to give expression to his emotions, he embraced her once more. He held his wife for a long, long moment, his arms tight around her.

Finally he remembered the figures and released her. "Shall we take these in the other room and christen our home?"

"Yes."

Together they walked through the house and he arranged her gift on one end of the mantel above the fireplace. "Until we have a permanent home in Nevada, we'll leave these here."

"We can live in your apartment. Now that we have this farmhouse to come to whenever we visit, I'm perfectly happy."

"I'm not." He hugged her around the waist. "We need a home. Before I left Reno, Zack handed me his wedding present. It's the deed to a parcel of land on his property near the Walker River, made out in both our names." Miguel paused. "Zack's the one who encouraged me to go after you—to find out if you loved me the way I loved you."

Her eyes misted over. "He's a true friend, Miguel."

"He's been offering me that land for years. When I told him I wouldn't take it, he begged me to buy it so we could be neighbors, as well as friends. But my life has been in too much turmoil, and I didn't want Zack mixed up in it. Now everything's changed and I'm a new man—because of you. Would you like to live there, Nickie? Shall we go back to Reno and start building our home?"

"Do you even have to ask?" Her face lit up, telling him everything he needed to know. "Since we both love the ranch, I can't imagine a better place to settle down and raise our family. The children will be able to grow up with horses and go riding with Zack's children and..." She threw out both arms in a spontaneous gesture of happiness. "Everything will be perfect!"

Miguel nodded.

"Irene and Fernando will be close by with their family. So will Andrew and Lindsay." He was referring to Governor Andrew Cordell, Zack's brother-in-law, and Lindsay, the woman he'd married a couple of years before.

Nickie smiled at him and reached out to touch his arm. "Your parents will be coming to visit, too, I hope. And mine, of course. And we'll have colleagues and students out to visit and—"

"What if I lose my tenure at the college?" Miguel asked abruptly.

"Would that be such a terrible thing?" she asked him in earnest. "You could be free to travel and accept speaking engagements. You've been tied to your job for a long time. This way you'd be able to help the Basque cause even more by accepting requests to lecture at various universities. You could spend more time on research, publish some original material. That's where your brilliance lies, Miguel, and I'd help you."

He cradled her face in his hands. "And what about *your* dreams of a career?"

"When I became your wife, I got what I wanted most in this life. The beauty of it is, I can still pursue my career goals because we're a team. Whether at work or home, we'll do everything together." She stood on tiptoe and brushed his lips with hers.

"And right now, I'm going to be the traditional Basque bride and fix you breakfast. I know perfectly well that no matter how many courses you ate at our wedding feast, you're hungry again."

"I am, but not for food."

"That's the first lie you've told me since I became your wife. I don't want to hear anymore."

Laughter rumbled out of him. "I'll let you do it on the condition that you'll allow me to watch."

"Just let me have a shower first." She flew across the room, picked up her suitcase and dashed into the bedroom, shutting the door.

After a quick shower, Nickie opened the suitcase and reached for a long cotton sweater and leggings. No sooner had she pulled them on than Miguel entered the room.

He looked tall and dark and powerful in his black velour bathrobe, and she found she couldn't take her eyes off him. Then it dawned on her that he'd brought them breakfast. She watched him put the tray on the dresser where her locket still lay.

Her gaze flicked to the two champagne glasses filled with pale gold liquid and a plate of delectable-looking tortillas, little omelets filled with potatoes and onions and eaten cold. Another plate held several slices of her favorite orange cake iced in marzipan, a local specialty.

He moved over to the door and closed it, then turned to her with a predatory gleam in his eyes. "I thought we'd have breakfast in bed," he murmured low in his throat.

"Miguel..."

"*Ez*, my beloved wife?"

"But I wanted to wait on *you*. You've given *me* everything."

"Not quite." In a few strides he reached the armoire and picked up a package she hadn't noticed until now. It looked as if it might be a picture. "Shall I open it for you?"

In her bemused state, a nod was all she could manage.

Within seconds the brown paper was removed and she stared at a large framed photograph of the meadow outside the farmhouse, vibrant with wildflowers, the mountain peaks in the background.

She couldn't move, couldn't speak. He must have sensed she was caught in the grip of overwhelming emotion because his eyes softened. "When summer comes, I'm going to make love to you in our meadow the way I longed to do years ago."

Her eyes searched his. "You *did* want me then."

"More than you'll ever know." His voice held a whisper of pain.

Nickie looked back at the photograph with eyes that glistened with tears. "We'll hang this over the mantel in the home we're going to build, and when our children ask us why..."

"...I'll tell them it's a secret between their mother and me."

They smiled at each other with the understanding that had bonded them from the beginning. Putting the picture down, he took a step toward her and she ran to embrace him—her future, her husband, the love of her heart.

HARLEQUIN ROMANCE®

Coming Next Month

#3327 ITALIAN INVADER Jessica Steele
Working for Max Zappelli has become more and more confusing for
Elyn Talbot. Her family believes he's responsible for the collapse of their
company, she believes he's an incorrigible womanizer, and he believes she's
a thief. And to complicate things further, Elyn is falling in love with the
irresistible Max.

#3328 THE DINOSAUR LADY Anne Marie Duquette
Jason Reilly *loves* dinosaurs. And he's crazy about Denver's Dinosaur Lady—
paleontologist and TV host Noel Forrest. He's actually got a fossil—he's *sure*
it's a dinosaur bone—to show Noel. He found it on Matt Caldwell's ranch,
where he's been going for recreational therapy ever since the accident that
left him crippled. Jason no longer has a family of his own, and he thinks Matt
and Noel would be the *perfect* parents for him. Now, if only he could get them
together....
This is our fourth Kids & Kisses title. Next month, watch for *Sullivan's Law*
by Amanda Clark.

#3329 THE CONFIRMED BACHELOR Ellen James
Rebecca Danley's a die-hard romantic. The way she figures it, you meet a
wonderful man, fall in love with him and want to have his kids...in that order.
Unfortunately, she's gotten things all turned around. She's become obsessed
with the idea of having children. Even worse, the only man in her life is a
confirmed bachelor!

#3330 AN IMPOSSIBLE KIND OF MAN Kay Gregory
Slade *was* impossible. Impossible to ignore! Especially now that Bronwen's
forced to share his apartment. But Bronwen still thinks she can ignore the
attraction she feels for him. And if the inevitable happens, she can always
count on Slade to do the honorable thing. *Can't she?*

AVAILABLE THIS MONTH:

#3323 AT ODDS WITH LOVE
Betty Neels

#3324 FAMILY SECRETS
Leigh Michaels

#3325 BRIDE OF MY HEART
Rebecca Winters

#3326 ON BLUEBERRY HILL
Marcella Thompson

Relive the romance... This September,
Harlequin and Silhouette are proud to bring you

by Request™

Marry Me... Again!

Some men are worth marrying *twice*...

Three complete novels by your favorite authors—
in one special collection!

FULLY INVOLVED by Rebecca Winters
FREE FALL by Jasmine Cresswell
MADE IN HEAVEN by Suzanne Simms

If you're looking to rekindle something wild, passionate
and unforgettable—then you're in luck.

Available wherever
Harlequin and Silhouette books are sold.

HARLEQUIN® Silhouette®

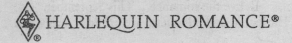

HARLEQUIN ROMANCE®

brings you

KIDS & KISSES

Stories that celebrate love, families and children!

Watch for our next Kids & Kisses title in September.

**The Dinosaur Lady
by Anne Marie Duquette
Harlequin Romance #3328**

A Romance that will move you and thrill you! By the author of **Rescued by Love, On the Line** *and* **Neptune's Bride.**

Noelle Forrest is "the Dinosaur Lady." Jason Reilly is the eleven-year-old boy who brings her a dinosaur fossil that may be her biggest career break ever—a fossil he found on Matt Caldwell's ranch.

Noelle discovers that there's room in her life and heart for more than just her career. There's room for Jason, who hasn't got a real family of his own—and for Matt, a strong compassionate man who thinks children are more important than dinosaurs....

Available wherever Harlequin books are sold.

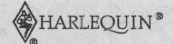

Harlequin Books requests the pleasure of your company this June in Eternity, Massachusetts, for WEDDINGS, INC.

For generations, couples have been coming to Eternity, Massachusetts, to exchange wedding vows. Legend has it that those married in Eternity's chapel are destined for a lifetime of happiness. And the residents are more than willing to give the legend a hand.

Beginning in June, you can experience the legend of Eternity. Watch for one title per month, across all of the Harlequin series.

HARLEQUIN BOOKS...
NOT THE SAME OLD STORY!

WEDGEN

FIC

Wu, William F.,
1951-

Warrior.

$4.99

DATE	BORROWER'S NAME	